TO MARRY A TIGER

by

ISOBEL CHACE

HARLEQUIN BOOKS

TORONTO
WINNIPEG

Original hard cover edtion published in 1971
by Mills & Boon Limited, 17 - 19 Foley Street,
London W1A 1DR, England

© Isobel Chace 1971

Harlequin edition published May, 1972

SBN 373-01586-0

Printed in Canada

1586

'. . . to marry a Sicilian must be something like marrying a tiger.'

A newspaper critic when Grasso
and his company gave a performance
of *Malia* in London

CHAPTER ONE

See Naples and die!

Ruth Arnold eased her feet out of her shoes and staggered over to the window of her hotel room. The view was every bit as wonderful as the brochures had promised. What they had not promised was the swarm of young men who had followed Ruth and her sister up and down every street ever since they had arrived. Pearl, who invariably felt at home in any kind of masculine society, had told Ruth that these were the famous 'little parrots' who made a habit of following female tourists, and who boasted much, but who actually achieved very little.

Very little as far as Ruth was concerned, she thought wryly. All she had collected had been a great number of bruising pinches. With Pearl it was different. Pearl had managed to find a different escort every night since their arrival, laughingly dismissing Ruth's warnings and reproaches as being just the sort of thing that Ruth would say. There had been Giulio, Giovanni, Marco, Pio, Rudolfo, and goodness knows how many more. And then there had been Mario.

Mario had edged his way into Ruth's life with a circumspection she did not generally associate with Italians. She had met him first in the muted lights of the hotel foyer, with Pearl, naturally, hanging on to his arm and drinking in his every word. Ruth hadn't caught his name, but had gathered that this was the Mario that Pearl had been talking about all day.

"You have a very pretty sister," he had smiled at Ruth.

Ruth had glared at him. For one thing he was far

too handsome and, for another, she hadn't liked the way he had looked at Pearl. Pearl was younger than she and, although she had always attracted boys like a honey-pot, she had no experience of anyone who might have wished to harm her.

"My mother used to say I was particularly well named!" Pearl had preened beside him. "Ruth had a different mother from mine," she had added inconsequentially.

Mario, who was tall in a way that Ruth found vaguely disturbing, had smiled faintly.

"That also is clear!" he had remarked.

No woman particularly likes being told she is plain, and Ruth was no exception. "My mother," she had retorted coldly, "was beautiful!"

Mario had said nothing. Ruth had seen the disbelief in his dark eyes and had hated the arrogant set to his features, made worse by his rather large nose which had been broken at one time, adding to his haughty, eagle-like expression.

"Ruth doesn't really remember her," Pearl had announced chattily. "She died, you see, and then Daddy married again, and that was *my* mother." She had sighed, looking somehow sad and sympathetic, although Ruth, who knew her very well, had known perfectly well that she had really been thinking about something quite different. "Mario darling, do let's go! Ruth doesn't *like* hanging around down here." She had giggled. "The young men annoy her! And anyway, she's tired!"

"Of course," Mario had purred.

Ruth had watched them go out, laughing together, and had felt as lonely as she had ever done. It was ridiculous, of course, for she wouldn't have wanted to go anywhere with this Mario. Not she! She could tell

8

at a glance what he was like—amusing himself where he could with that mild, smug contempt that he obviously had for all her sex.

Now she stared out of the hotel bedroom window across the famous bay, and prickled with anxiety for Pearl. Mario was no boy to be teased and slapped down at her youthful whim. Mario was a man, and a dangerous man at that!

Ruth sighed. It was already getting dark, she noticed. They were going to have another of those vivid, dramatic sunsets that she had come to look for each evening. The full moon, a heavy, burnished gold disc in the sky, was already struggling across the darkened horizon, taking over the lighting of the Bay from the waning sun. It was a warm, romantic night that asked for trouble. Ruth shivered faintly. If only Pearl were less of a tease. If only she knew what she was doing when she teased and tempted someone as ruthless and volatile as this man Mario. If only—! But she wasn't. Pearl was a darling, but there was no doubt that she was the original innocent abroad and was heading straight for trouble! And she, Ruth, would be responsible! For it was she who had decided that Pearl should go with her as she used her summer holidays in a leisurely discovery of ancient Rome. She pursed her lips thoughtfully, wondering a little at her own motives. It hadn't only been because she rather enjoyed the bubbling personality of her young sister, she had also been shocked that Pearl had no interest in anything outside her own immediate circle of masculine acquaintances. Why, it was doubtful that she had even heard of Julius Caesar, let alone any of the other great figures of the past who had set their mark on history right down to the present day!

But Pearl's response to Italy had not been to broaden her mind, but merely to broaden her circle of male admirers. Ruth had tried not to mind the times she had been left on her own, evening after evening, but she did mind Pearl's hectic admiration for this Mario. She had disliked him before she had met him and she had seen nothing in him to make her change her mind. There was no doubt about it, Pearl was in danger! The problem was how to extricate her from Mario's talons, without actually taking her home to her mother in disgrace. For that was one thing that Pearl would not readily forgive. It was bad enough, she had remarked on many an occasion, for Ruth to be a schoolmistress, without her playing the part at home. It was one of the few things that Pearl never laughed about. In her opinion, Ruth was little short of a traitor for joining the ranks of an army of autocrats against whom Pearl had waged relentless war for the whole of her school-days.

Ruth sighed again. What was she to do? She changed her clothes with a worried frown creasing her forehead. Perhaps she should talk to Pearl? Or perhaps she could suggest that they went on to Amalfi? No, that wouldn't do, Amalfi was far too near Naples and Mario! Bother the man! Surely he could find someone else to amuse him for a few days!

She went downstairs to her lonely hotel dinner, clutching her room key to her in case she lost it, annoyed with herself because she hated going into the large, impersonal room by herself, knowing that the waiters pitied her because they guessed that she ate so sparingly, not because she wasn't hungry, but because every moment was an agony to her. Accordingly, she meekly accepted the dish of spaghetti that the waiter produced for her, although she was reasonably sure that she had ordered nothing of the sort. It was, she decided, quite exceptionally good, and she cast the waiter a grateful smile that she instantly regretted when it was returned by a warm, knowing wink. The colour slid up into her cheeks and she was instantly quite wildly angry with Pearl. This was no city for any female to tackle alone if she were in her early twenties and even only bearably good-looking.

She had almost finished her meal and was trying to decide whether it was worth delaying her departure from the dining room to have some coffee when Pearl came flying into the room and sat down opposite her, her whole face alight with excitement.

"What do you think, Ruth? Mario says we must go to Sicily—"

"Why?" Ruth countered suspiciously.

"Because he *comes* from Sicily! He *lives* there! And he wants me to see his home. Don't you think it's kind of him?"

"No, I don't," Ruth retorted frankly.

Pearl blinked. Ruth found herself wishing that her sister would not wear false eyelashes, they looked so black and unnatural against her very fair skin. Perhaps if she were to trim them to a proper shape they would look a little better?

"But he'll pay!" Pearl explained with fervour. "He wants to see me against the background of the house, you see."

"I see exactly," Ruth said with some asperity. "Really, Pearl! You can't be so silly that you don't see what he really wants!"

Pearl had the grace to blush. "I think you're mean," she said with a sob. "Mario isn't like that at all!"

"Then tell me what he is like!" Ruth snapped.

Pearl's face took on a dreamy quality and her bright blue eyes filled with tears. "He's wonderful!" she breathed.

Ruth bit her lip. "Pearl, I don't want to lecture you—" she began.

"Then don't!" Pearl advised her promptly.

"I have to!" Ruth insisted. "Don't you see *why* he wants to take us to Sicily?"

"It isn't really us," Pearl pouted. "He asked me on my own!"

"Well, there you are, then!" Ruth rallied. "Surely that made you wonder why?"

Pearl shook her head. "No, it didn't. I *know* why he asked me! If I fit in with his home—and everything—he'll ask me to marry him!"

Ruth was unfeeling enough to chuckle. "Don't be silly, dear," she advised phlegmatically.

Pearl sobbed quietly to herself. "You don't understand Italians at all!" she complained. "They're not dull and uninteresting enough for your taste and so you don't like them!"

Ruth's amusement died. "I'm trying to tell you that Mario's code of behaviour is not the same as ours," she said helplessly.

"It's better!" Pearl informed her quickly. "The Sicilian code of honour is world-famous!"

"World-*infamous*!" Ruth corrected her.

"Oh, *Ruth*!" Pearl giggled.

"Well, so it is!" Ruth went on, nettled by her sister's unashamed laughter. "If a man wants to marry a girl, all he has to do is compromise her. She can be engaged to a hundred other men for all he cares, society, the law, *everything,* forces her into a marriage she doesn't want and which can't possibly make her happy! *And*," she added darkly, "they have the audacity to say it's because of the girl's honour!"

Pearl's blue eyes grew round and interested. "Well?" she demanded.

"There was a case in the paper just the other day," Ruth went on. "The poor girl refused to marry this young man and he gave her the choice; she could either marry him or he would kill her! She had to have police protection. Even her family said she had been dishonoured and should marry him."

"And did she?" Pearl asked.

Ruth was obliged to admit that she didn't know. "But you couldn't imagine such a thing happening in England, could you?" she said.

"No!" Pearl breathed. She cast Ruth such a blithely innocent look that her sister began to wonder what plot she could possibly be hatching now. She had met the same look frequently before and, in her experience, it invariably meant trouble. "I wonder if Mario would worry about my honour," Pearl went on happily.

"I doubt it!" Ruth said quickly.

"So do I!" Pearl confessed with a pretty giggle. "But he would care about his own honour. The Verdecchios are a very old Sicilian family—he's always going on about what his ancestors did centuries and centuries ago!"

Ruth felt a brief stirring of interest, but she repressed it quickly. Mario was of no possible interest to her!

"I daresay," she said in answer to her sister. "But I don't suppose for a minute he'd think that there was anything dishonourable in—in—" She sought vainly for the right word that would warn Pearl without frightening her.

"Despoiling an innocent English girl?" Pearl supplied, her eyes dancing. "Oh, Ruth! You're positively Victorian!"

Ruth, who knew a great deal more about the seamier side of Victorian life than Pearl, smiled wearily. "So, I suspect, is he!" she said dryly.

Pearl looked puzzled, then her brow cleared magically. "I suppose you mean that he polishes off young females by the dozen!" she sighed. She put her elbows on the table and supported her head in her hands.

"He's terribly romantic, isn't he? You know, Ruth, I think it might be *fun*—"

"Well, I don't!" Ruth exclaimed hastily. "Pearl, you're not to go with him! Promise me you won't!"

Pearl giggled. "Worse than Victorian!" she teased. "You're positively Gothic!"

'But you do promise?" Ruth insisted anxiously.

Pearl's innocent blue eyes met hers. "I promise he won't have *everything* his own way!" she gurgled. "Will that do?"

Ruth looked at her young sister. She felt her misgivings like a physical weight on her shoulders, but she doubted if she would get anything more out of Pearl. She felt a little prick of envy as she thought how nice it must be if the whole of life appeared as nothing more than a pleasant romantic adventure. "I suppose it will have to," she said dully.

Pearl nibbled happily at a lump of sugar she had found on the table. "Don't look so sad, darling!" She cast Ruth an ecstatic smile. "I'm not compromised yet! And it may never happen!"

Not yet! Ruth sniffed. Certainly not yet! But she wished she could rid herself of the conviction that it was only a matter of time!

"Shall we go home?" she suggested suddenly, a flame of hope flashing through her.

Pearl had the grace to feel ashamed. "I wish you wouldn't worry so!" she said quite crossly. "If the truth were told, you know, I can take care of myself a great deal better than you can."

But Ruth didn't believe her. Pearl was nothing more than a romantic innocent, fresh from school, whereas Ruth had earned her own living for the last three years and had the usual scars of living to show for it. How could Pearl know what men like Mario were like? Ruth's own experience might not be very extensive, but

14

her young sister's was non-existent! And Ruth was quite certain that she had not imagined that gleam in Mario's eye. Pearl might think what she would, but Ruth knew better than to suppose that he would allow himself to be worsted by a slip of a girl!

Pearl went on a shopping expedition the next morning. Ruth was not sorry that she wanted to go alone, for she found these endless trips round the hot stores quite exhausting.

"What will you do?" Pearl had asked her as she was waiting for her taxi.

"I think I'll stay here," Ruth had answered.

Pearl's eyes had danced with laughter. "Aren't you afraid I'll be captured by the big, bad wolf?" she had asked.

Ruth had found it far from being a laughing matter. "You haven't arranged to meet him, have you?" she had asked baldly.

Pearl had giggled in the most maddening way. "Not this morning!" she had said with her tongue in her cheek. "I wouldn't be wearing this old thing if I had!" she had added disparagingly, glaring at her practically new coat in a way that Ruth found far more convincing than any amount of protestations would have done.

Pearl had gone, dancing into the taxi as gay as a bird. Ruth, on the other hand, had stopped in the foyer of the hotel, brooding over her sister's affairs for fully an hour before she had pulled herself together sufficiently to go up to the desk and ask if there were any letters for them.

"Miss Arnold," the Italian receptionist repeated, pleased to show off his excellent English. "There is one here for Miss Arnold."

Ruth peered at the envelope. "It doesn't say if it's for my sister or for me," she said doubtfully.

"That is easily answered," the Italian smiled. "I think I am correct in thinking you are the elder sister, is that not so? Then *you* are Miss Arnold. Your sister is Miss Pearl Arnold," he added dreamily. "She is well named, if you will forgive my saying so!"

"Then you think this letter is for me?" Ruth prompted him.

"Most certainly."

She thanked him, turning the envelope over in her hands. It was not for her. She knew that immediately, for no one in Italy would be writing to her and the letter had an Italian stamp. She tried to see the postmark, but it was too blurred to read. She thought it said Sicily, but she couldn't be sure.

With the letter still in her hand, she took the lift up to her room. The writing was firmly masculine, uncompromising and unadorned. Supposing it was Mario? she thought with a prickle of alarm. But why should he write to Pearl when he was here in Naples?

She turned the envelope over again, staring down at it. It was clearly addressed to Miss Arnold, so she had every right to open it. The receptionist had said it was for her. If only she didn't really know perfectly well that it was intended for Pearl, she wouldn't have hesitated.

There would be no harm, of course, in opening the envelope and looking inside. If the letter were addressed to Pearl she wouldn't dream of reading it. She would put it on her sister's bed and explain to her what the receptionist had said. It wouldn't sound particularly convincing, but Pearl seldom explored anyone else's motives for what they did. She would probably be only too pleased not to have to go to the trouble of opening the letter for herself.

Ruth slipped a nail-file into the envelope and slit it open. It was a very bulky letter for a simple missive, she thought. She pulled out the contents and laid them flat on the table in front of her.

"Beloved," she read. *That* was certainly intended for Pearl, but there was nothing whatever to say so. "The boat leaves tonight. All you have to do is to get your passport from the clerk and take a taxi to the dock. I'll be waiting for you at Palermo. Sicily will welcome you with open arms, as also do I, Mario."

For a long moment, Ruth stared through unseeing eyes at the piece of paper in front of her. How dared he! And how dared Pearl! She thought wildly how she could pay him back for his bland confidence that Pearl would rush to do his bidding. Well, the Arnolds were built of sterner stuff than he had imagined! And it would give her the very greatest pleasure to prove it to him! But how?

She put the letter down, ripping the envelope in her anxiety to discover what else it contained. There was a boat ticket, she saw, noting with a flicker of contempt that it was a first-class ticket, such as a man might be expected to get for the bird he was charming at that particular moment. There was also, Ruth found, a great deal of money. The enormous, crisp notes were of denominations that made her gasp. Even allowing for the fact that Italian lire came in thousands before they were worth anything at all, it was a very considerable sum of money indeed. The sight of it sent the colour flying to her cheeks. How dared he! she thought with considerable agitation. How dared he! Why, it was as if he had already bought and paid for Pearl just as he might any other commodity. Only he hadn't bought Pearl yet, whatever he might care to think!

By the end of the morning a plan of action had formed itself in Ruth's mind. Mario Verdecchio was an abomination and he would get no more than he deserved if his plans went awry! He might be able to charm Pearl into doing—*anything*, but she, Ruth, was a very different cup of tea!

The receptionist was pleased to see her when she went to the desk to ask for her passport.

"The letter, it was for you?" he asked her.

She nodded gravely. "Miss Arnold," she confirmed.

"And here is your passport," he smiled at her. "Will you take them both?"

Ruth was seized by a sudden doubt as to whether she was doing the right thing. "N-no," she managed. "My sister won't need hers. I—I have to have mine for the bank."

"But of course," the clerk agreed.

Ruth sighed with relief as she left the desk. It was all being so very much easier than she had expected. All she had to do was to behave quite normally for the rest of the day. It was so simple!

She had to admit that Pearl made it easier for her than she could have hoped for. The younger girl rushed into the hotel for a quick lunch, apologetically explaining that she had a date for the rest of the day. "That is," she had said suddenly, "if there isn't a letter for me. Did you ask at the desk?"

"There was nothing for Miss Pearl Arnold."

"What a funny way of saying no! I suppose you got something?" It was typical of Pearl that she didn't inquire any further. She was supremely uninterested in the affairs of anyone other than herself.

And then she had gone in a flurry. Ruth had almost called her back, but Pearl had only waved at her, running to meet the pale, black-haired youth who was waiting for her on the corner of the street.

Ruth packed her bag with care, wishing that she didn't feel so guilty. What she was doing she was doing to help Pearl, and yet she couldn't help feeling that Pearl wasn't going to like it. Still, no matter what, she wasn't going to allow Mario Verdecchio to get away with it easily. She would show him!

She was extremely nervous by the time the taxi arrived to take her to the ship. She paid her bill at the desk and left a note for Pearl, explaining to her what she had done. The few words that she had written to her sister had taken her most of the afternoon to compose, for there was no doubt about it, Pearl was going to be very angry indeed. It took all Ruth's resolution to go through with the thing in the end. She was quite sure that Mario would do nothing to hurt her, that there was nothing to it really. All she had to do was to get on the boat and disembark at Palermo the next morning. By the next morning she would be back in Naples with the satisfaction of knowing that she had told Mario exactly what she thought of him.

The taxi drove through Naples at a great pace. Ruth took a last look at the numerous cafés that surrounded the Bay and the tall, dusty trees that gave them shade. For some reason she had the feeling that she would never see any of it ever again.

"That's your ship," the taxi-driver told her, pointing it out amidst the huge liners that crowded the dock on either side.

Ruth thanked him, giving him a handsome tip as he placed her luggage on the concrete beside her. He gave her a cheerful grin and disappeared, leaving her alone in a sea of strangers all gesticulating and shouting at one another as they pressed into the small office that dealt with their tickets and arranged for the cars to be taken on board by crane.

Ruth took her place in the queue with increased misgivings. She didn't like the way the men stared at her and she wished, hopelessly, that she were not travelling alone, a fact which seemed to be more than enough to set them speculating about her.

19

When at last her turn came an official glanced at her ticket, stamped it and gave it back to her.

"You may go on board, *signorina*," he told her.

Ruth took a deep breath. It was too late now to turn back. She was on her way to Sicily!

There was another woman already in the double cabin when she went below decks to find her way round the ship. She was small, dumpy, and very dark, but she spoke English reasonably well and seemed friendly.

"Are you going to Tunis?" she asked Ruth.

"No, only to Palermo," Ruth answered.

"I go to Tunis," the dumpy little woman informed her. "But tomorrow I spend in Palermo. I visit my nephew there. The ship stays all day, so it is easy for me."

"I suppose you have been there often," Ruth suggested as she unpacked the few things she would need for the night.

"Often and often!" The older woman gave Ruth a kindly look. "You travel alone?"

Ruth nodded. "I'm being met at Palermo," she mumbled.

"Sicily is beautiful. To me it is going home!" The Italian woman sighed. "Now, I live in Tunis with my husband, but I cannot return to Sicily too often. You are fortunate to be staying there." She glanced at the label on Ruth's luggage. "Miss Arnold? I am Signora Verdecchio."

Ruth felt distinctly weak at the knees. "Did you say Verdecchio?" she asked weakly.

"You have heard the name before?" the Signora demanded sharply.

Ruth nodded.

The Italian woman sparkled. "You must know my

nephew!" she explained in triumph. "It is Mario, is it not?" Ruth nodded again. "Dear Mario! Do you go to meet *him* in Palermo?" Mario's aunt added by way of an appalled afterthought.

Ruth nodded a third time, quite unable to speak.

"*Mario!*" The Italian woman blinked at her. "You plan to *marry* him?"

"Oh no!" Ruth was glad to be able to sound quite positive about something. "I hardly know him."

Signora Verdecchio looked confused. "Then why do you go to Sicily? Is it—is it *that* kind of an arrangement?"

Ruth could feel herself blushing. "No, it's nothing like that!" she protested.

"No?" The Italian woman sank on to her bunk. She gave Ruth a long searching look and apparently decided that she was telling the truth. Ruth was pretty enough, but she certainly wasn't flamboyant enough to appeal to Mario, that much was obvious!

"I think," she said at last, "you had better tell me all about it, no?"

Ruth did not relish the prospect, but Mario's aunt had a very determined expression and she was reasonably sure that she meant to have the story either from herself, here and now, or from her nephew in the morning. On the whole the former seemed the preferable course, and so she stammered out the whole story.

"So," the Signora said when she was finished. "It was this Pearl that Mario invited to Sicily." Her eyes danced with sudden amusement. "And he paid the ticket, you say?"

"It came to me because I am the elder," Ruth explained uncomfortably.

"But of course it came to you!" Mario's aunt agreed firmly. "And now you are not to worry your head any further about it tonight!" She choked on her own laughter. "But tomorrow—tomorrow we will give Mario a nice surprise, no?"

Ruth hung her head. "I don't think he will be very pleased," she said.

But the older woman only laughed again. "It will be very amusing for all of us!" she insisted. "And you need not worry about Mario! *I* will manage him!" And she looked so determined about it that Ruth very nearly believed her.

CHAPTER TWO

WHEN Ruth awoke in the morning the engines were already still. Ruth looked over to where Mario's aunt had been sleeping, but she had already dressed and gone up on deck. Ruth hurried into her clothes and re-packed the few things she had needed during the night. Through the porthole she could see the sunlight dancing on the water and she was more than a little excited at the thought of seeing a new place and one that she had always wanted to visit.

Signora Verdecchio greeted her gaily when she went up on deck.

"Can you see Mario?" she asked her. "He always comes to meet me when I pass through, but I can't see him anywhere."

Ruth's spirits sank at the mere mention of his name, but she obediently studied the waiting figures on the dock, looking for the tall, arrogant form of Mario Verdecchio. However, there was no sign of him anywhere.

"I expect we'll find him at the bottom of the gangway," the Signora said comfortably. "I have to get a ticket to come back on board this evening and then we'll get ashore." She went off to look for the steward, waving her passport back and forth in front of his nose.

Ruth stood in the background while the wave of excited Italian broke over her. It seemed to her that both the Signora and the steward were extremely angry about something, and she hoped that it wasn't anything to do with her.

"It is Mario!" the Signora said with extreme annoyance when she had finished with the steward. "The steward had a message for me from him. I shall have to travel to Messina to see an old friend who has fallen sick—"

"So you won't be seeing Mario?" Ruth broke in, feeling slightly sick.

"I'll look in on my way back," the Signora promised. "There's nothing to get upset about. Whatever Mario has planned, he can hardly do anything to you before this evening."

"N-no," Ruth agreed uncertainly. She wished she hadn't come.

"I'll see you tonight," the Signora smiled gently, her eyes anxious as she thought of her friend. "You have nothing to worry about!"

Ruth watched Mario's aunt trip lightly down the gangway and turn and wave to her. She waved back, annoyed with herself, for she was afraid she was going to cry. She forced herself to look at what she could see of the island. The city shone white in the morning sun and it was possible to hear the hum of noise that came from the streets clearly from the ship. It was not, perhaps, quite so beautiful as Naples, but Ruth found it infinitely preferable. The heat was as unbearable and oppressive as the Italian summer could make it, but whereas in Naples the noise and confusion merely added to the heat, here she could feel a soft breeze and there was a faint smell of lemons to encourage her.

The steward brought up her luggage and hurried her ashore, anxious not to lose his tip to any of the porters who might have come streaming aboard if anyone had wanted them. Ruth stood uncertainly at the bottom of the gangway, wondering what she ought to do next. There was still no sign of Mario.

A long time went by and still no one had approached Ruth. She began to think that she should make enquiries as to where Mario Verdecchio lived, but she could think of no way of making herself understood, so she abandoned the idea. She was just picking up her suitcase and walking away from the ship towards a café she could see about a hundred yards away, when a uniformed man came up to her, his black eyes full of apology.

"Are you Miss Arnold?" he asked in English.

She turned in relief. "Yes. Yes, I am," she admitted.

He smiled, showing a glint of gold in his teeth. "I am to drive you to Signor Verdecchio's house," he said.

He grasped her suitcase and strode over to a large black limousine. Ruth had never seen such a car before. It had a green window in the front to make driving in the hot sun more bearable, and blinds that effectively hid the occupants inside from the rear and sides. The chauffeur opened the door for her and ushered her into the spacious, extremely comfortable rear seat.

"Signor Verdecchio told me to expect a very fair lady," he went on apologetically. "That is why I didn't immediately recognise you. I am very sorry."

Ruth thought wryly that it was hardly his fault if he had not recognised her from a description of Pearl. Ruth was fair too, but she had none of the fragile, ashen-blonde look of Pearl. Ruth was taller and stronger and, in her face lacked Pearl's prettiness, her features were firmer and full of character.

The chauffeur drove straight through Palermo, heading for the hills beyond. Ruth peered out at the narrow streets, full of tall buildings where everyone seemed to live on their balconies, even doing their shopping by shouting down to the vendors in the street.

"Do the people sleep on the balconies as well as everything else?" Ruth asked the chauffeur.

He laughed. "Everything is *sub coelo* in Sicily," he told her. "It is too hot indoors. Even the hens prefer the balconies in this weather! And why not?"

Ruth smiled. "It looks a bit crowded," she commented.

The chauffeur shrugged his shoulders. "It is convenient. The women can gossip, the men can watch the world go by. What more do you want?"

There was so much to look at that Ruth had to lean right forward to see everything. Some main roads had been cut right through the old city to take the main burden of the traffic and which looked much the same as any of the other main roads she had seen in Milan, Turin, or any other big centre. But away from these main roads, the city was just as it had always been. The houses were peculiarly foreign to Ruth's English eye. They were solid and compact, all of them painted in pale colours, and without either chimneys or spires on the churches. In those houses of which she got a glimpse as they passed, there were tiled floors, and every window seemed to be equipped with Venetian blinds. The whole atmosphere was one of cheerful business which Ruth found extremely attractive.

The Verdecchio house was out in the country. They came to a small village that lay between rich vineyards and drove the whole length of the small street that separated the houses of the people. At the far end were some heavy wrought-iron gates that had been left open. They swept through the gates and up a lengthy tree-lined drive that was covered with yellow dust and a few straggly weeds that fought for a poor living in the shade of the trees. The house stood far back from the road. It was large with painted shuttered windows and a great deal of wrought-iron work round the windows and doorways. Huge, colourful bushes spread themselves over some large flower beds in front of the house and a few citrus trees thrived at the other end of what was meant to be a lawn, but which actually had little in common with its vivid green English equivalent.

The chauffeur drew up outside the front door and held the door of the car for her to get out. Ruth stood on the drive and looked about her. There was no sign of anyone anywhere.

"I suppose they are expecting me?" she said nervously.

"I will ring the bell!" the chauffeur answered. He did so, pulling on an ancient knob that let loose a grand peal somewhere in the depths of the house.

"Giulia will look after you now," he said with satisfaction. He placed her suitcase beside her in the doorway and saluted smartly. "Signor Verdecchio will have left instructions," he added.

Ruth wondered if there was anyone there to answer the bell. She pulled at the knob as the chauffeur had done, but the only answer was silence. When she had satisfied herself that no one was coming, she decided to walk round the house to see if there was any other entrance. A like house in the depths of the English countryside, she thought, could always be approached from the rear sooner than from the front: perhaps in Sicily it was just the same?

The house was even larger than she had imagined. There were some stables set at right angles to the main building in which she could hear some horses moving restively and a donkey braying. A small dog came running out to greet her. He was of no known variety, small and button-eyed, with a proud tail that he waved behind him like a flag. Ruth bent down to say hullo and the animal graciously allowed her to approach and to tickle the back of his head.

"Are you a Verdecchio too?" she asked him.

The dog waved his tail and led the way round the house to the back door just as a large woman emerged from the vegetable garden.

"Giulia?" Ruth exclaimed in relief.

The woman stared at her crossly. She ripped out half a dozen questions in Italian, so fast that Ruth had no hope of understanding her.

"Signor Mario Verdecchio?" she asked patiently.

The woman nodded, her whole face breaking into smiles. She beckoned to Ruth to follow her into the house, chattering away as they went. Signor Verdecchio had had to go away, but he had left instructions about the English lady who was to come to Sicily. She was to be made welcome and a bedroom was to be prepared for her. She, Giulia, was to serve her with food and to see to her comfort. And so she would, for there was no one within a hundred miles for whom she would rather work than for the Signor. He was a man!

Ruth looked so doubtful that the Italian woman was sure that she hadn't understood her properly. She gave Ruth a sly nudge in the ribs and laughed. The English lady probably knew more about Signor Verdecchio than she did, wasn't that so?

Stony-faced, Ruth refused to acknowledge that she had understood the innuendo.

"Where is Signor Verdecchio?" she asked coldly.

"At the bedside of a friend of his," Giulia replied, a little unsure of this strange English woman. "He is over at Messina. He will be back soon enough."

Ruth certainly hoped so. She didn't want to stay any longer at the Verdecchio house than she could help.

"Perhaps I could make myself a cup of coffee," she suggested gently.

Giulia bridled. "I will bring it to you in the *salotto*, if you will wait there."

She almost pushed Ruth before her, through the kitchen and across a wide, elegant terrace. The sitting room, full of austere and awkward furniture, was reached through a large casement window.

"Wait here," Giulia commanded grimly.

Ruth sat nervously on the edge of an elegant *chaise-longue* and wondered bitterly how she was expected to fill in her time before the infamous Mario deigned to come home and meet her. It was strange how he had the ability to make her angry whatever he did! She had never known anyone else who made her prickle with sheer temper when he had done nothing more than compare her unfavourably with Pearl's ash-blonde prettiness—and at least twenty other men had done that! But then they hadn't looked at her with quite the same cynical amusement that had so exasperated her!

There were a few books on a table by the telephone and Ruth went across the room to take a closer look at them. Only one was in English, an American novel that she had already read. Ruth picked it up nevertheless and began to leaf through the pages to see if she remembered the story as well as she thought she did.

The telephone rang shrilly beside her, making her jump. She hesitated for a minute, then she picked up the receiver.

"That you, Mario?" a particularly English voice said in her ear.

"No," she stammered back. "I'm afraid he's out."

There was a lengthy pause, in which she could almost hear the Englishman's surprise.

"Who are you?" the voice asked.

"Miss Arnold. Ruth Arnold."

"Arnold?" There was a faint chuckle. "Are you the Pearl Beyond Price?"

Ruth blushed. "No, I am not," she said distinctly.

More laughter. "I'm coming over to find out!" the voice informed her. "Mario has no right to keep you to himself anyway."

Ruth tried to sound sophisticated and cool. "Suit yourself," she said. She put the receiver back on its cradle and wished she were dead. It had all been so simple back in Naples. She would teach Mario a lesson and that would be that. She hadn't thought that other people might complicate matters, or that Mario *wouldn't even be there to meet her!*

Giulia came running into the room, a cup of steaming coffee in one hand.

"Did you hear the telephone?" she asked unnecessarily.

Ruth nodded. "It was an Englishman," she said.

Giulia gave the telephone a knowing look. "That will be the Signor Brett," she muttered.

"He's coming over," Ruth added.

"Did you tell him Signor Verdecchio is away for the day?"

Ruth smiled slowly. "I think he is coming over to see me," she said.

"It is your business," Giulia acknowledged. "But the Signor Verdecchio will not be pleased. This man, Henry Brett, he serves the Signor. He works on his land, laying pipes for water. *He* doesn't share his leisure-time—"

"Perhaps you will bring a cup of coffee for him when he comes," Ruth interrupted her.

"Signor Verdecchio will not like it!" Giulia snapped. "He did not bring you here for Signor Brett!"

Ruth held her head high. "I came of my own accord," she said. "And I'll do what I like!"

Giulia's eyes glittered. "I will tell Signor Verdecchio—"

"Signor Verdecchio already knows!" Ruth cut her off curtly and quite untruthfully. "Please show Mr. Brett in here when he comes."

With a grudging look of respect for Ruth, Giulia set down the cup of coffee and left the room. It was very quiet when she had gone. Ruth walked restlessly up and down the room, looking at this and that just to fill in time. There were several dark portraits on the walls, she noticed. Some of them had a distinct look of Mario, cynical and forbidding, with a touch of the hauteur she so despised in him. They were probably, she thought indifferently, his ancestors who had lived in the house before him.

That it was a very ancient house, she had no doubt. The Moorish arches and the fountain that played on the corner of the terrace spoke silently of the Sicilian past, when the island had been a part of the great Arab civilisation that had stretched from one end of the Mediterranean to the other. Some of the material that had been used to build the arches were older still, with Roman capitals, some of them still bearing the legend of the names of the ancient gods of Rome.

Indeed, the house was so full of history that Mario had scarcely impressed his own personality at all. The discovery gave Ruth great satisfaction. Why should she be afraid of such a man? Not that she was, she told herself hurriedly, but it was nice to know that in some ways he was so nondescript.

Mr. Brett's arrival was announced by the dog. Ruth could hear him barking long before Giulia brought him in to the sitting room with glowering disapproval. Ruth rose to her feet and smiled at the stranger.

"Mr. Brett?" she asked hesitantly.

He was a man in his middle thirties, she judged,

although his hair was already turning grey. His skin was of the very fair kind that refuses to tan, but goes scarlet in the sun, and the backs of his hands were a mass of freckles ending in unkempt nails that had apparently seen a great deal of hard labour. His green eyes smiled at her.

"No, I can see at a glance that you are not Pearl after all!" he said regretfully.

"Pearl is my sister," Ruth told him.

He looked surprised. "I hadn't thought that Mario had intended to bring the whole family!"

"He didn't," Ruth retorted.

Mr. Brett looked amused and faintly respectful. "Does he know you're here?" he asked.

She shook her head. "Not yet," she said grimly.

Mr. Brett emitted a long whistle. "Sooner you than me!" he exclaimed.

Ruth sat down with dignity. "I prefer not to discuss it," she told him. "What are you doing in Sicily, Mr. Brett?"

He raised his eyebrows a little at her sudden formality. "I'm putting in an irrigation system on Mario's estate," he answered her. "We hope it's going to do great things for the local people. They're not as poor as some of the people in Sicily—Mario has seen to that!—but the old, grinding poverty is only just below the surface."

"And how will irrigation help?" Ruth enquired, suddenly very glad to have someone to talk to.

"It'll help," he said briefly. "They'll lose less of their topsoil for a start. It'll mean they can have water piped to their houses too."

"D'you mean they haven't water now?" Ruth asked, appalled.

"They share a tap at the end of the street. Would you like to see what we're doing for yourself?"

Ruth was immediately enthusiastic. "May I?" she said. "Can we go now?"

He smiled lazily. "I don't see why not. You can come back to my place for lunch if you'd care to?"

"I'd love it!" she exclaimed. "Mr. Brett—"

"Call me Henry," he interposed lazily.

The easy colour fled up Ruth's cheeks. "My name is Ruth," she said awkwardly.

"How apt!" he commented.

She was surprised. "Why do you say that?" she asked him. Nobody had ever suggested that her name was in the least bit like her before, not in the same way as Pearl was like her name, with her ash-blonde hair and fair, creamy skin.

Henry Brett laughed. "I don't know. Ruth amidst the alien corn and all that sort of thing, I suppose."

She smiled too. "Only there is no Boaz for me to set my cap at," she said gruffly.

His green eyes opened very wide. "I rather thought Mario was already cast for the part," he murmured.

Ruth looked shocked. "Certainly not," she said. "I hardly know him."

Henry laughed a good deal at that. "It isn't always considered necessary!" he remarked dryly.

"It is with me!" Ruth claimed in a voice that quivered despite her. Why, she didn't even *like* Mario, and besides, she had Pearl's feelings to consider. She had come to Sicily to punish Mario, not to compete with her sister for his favours.

Henry smiled down at her. "Come on," he said. "I'll show you over the estate."

Henry Brett drove a jeep that was old enough to have been left over from the last war. Its hard canvas seats were ingrained with the dirt of the years, giving the vehicle a seedy look that fitted in well with the surrounding scenery. The land was a hard land. It was dry and dusty, with the occasional olive tree to give an illusion of wealth. Sometimes the rock came right

33

through the tired topsoil to break the old-fashioned ploughs that were still dragged through the dust at planting time. Some long-legged sheep nibbled for a living where they could, watched over by a sleeping youth who was hiding his head from the heat of the sun.

"Have a good look," Henry said to Ruth. "You'll see the difference then where the scheme is already in operation."

"Where is that?" Ruth asked.

He pointed into the distance. "On the other side of the village," he said.

It seemed to Ruth that Mario owned an awful lot of land. Odd, semi-deserted houses peppered the fields, but most of the people had been gathered into the newer houses that huddled together in the village. From a distance it looked as though the houses were falling over one another in their anxiety to reach the top of the hill, their pantiled roofs and white-painted façades leaning at crazy angles one to the other.

Henry drove the jeep straight up the single, narrow cobbled street with an open drain that ran down the centre, carrying away the water from the women's washing and the litter of the day's marketing. In the centre of the village was a square built round a fountain that only played in wet weather, and the church that was the centre of almost everything.

On the other side of the village, it was true, the grass grew greener, the vines were weighed down with fruit, and the animals were sleeker and fatter.

"You see!" Henry grinned in triumph. "That's what water will do for you!"

"Where does it come from?"

"A nearby lake." Henry's interest wavered. "Tell me, Ruth, what do you do at home in England?"

"Me?" Ruth was curiously flattered that he should be interested enough in her to ask. "I teach," she said.

34

He stuck his tongue into his cheek. "I never would have guessed!" he said solemnly. "Teach what?"

"History mostly," she told him. "That's why Pearl and I came to Italy. I've always longed to see these places for myself!"

"And now you have?" he said gently.

"Some of them. I haven't seen anything here yet. Did you know that it was by a lake in Sicily that Proserpina disappeared when Pluto captured her? It must have been somewhere around here that Ceres started searching for her."

"Is Ceres the same person as Demeter?"

Ruth nodded. "Demeter is her Greek, and Ceres her Roman name," she explained.

"And she found her lost daughter in the underworld? But the poor girl could only surface for half the year? Is that the right story?"

Ruth smiled. "It makes you think when it all happened around here," she said earnestly.

"You almost sound as if you believed it!" Henry exclaimed.

"I suppose I do, in a way," she admitted. "Not the story exactly," she went on hurriedly, "but the poetic idea."

Henry stared at her. "You've lost me!" he admitted. "You'd better keep that kind of remark for Mario. He goes in for legends and history too. Me, I'm a modern kind of individual bringing water to real people who are living here and now."

Ruth chuckled. "There wouldn't be any rain for you to use if Ceres hadn't cried over the loss of her daughter!"

Henry shook his head. "I never thought of that!" he admitted. "It's a pity she didn't cry a bit more, that's all I can say!"

35

Ruth enjoyed that day more than any other day she had spent in Italy. She had found it fascinating to watch Henry's mechanical diggers laying the deep trenches through which the piped water went. She had liked to watch the gangs of sun-darkened men who were working on the scheme. Most of them wore jaunty, bright yellow crash helmets, and all of them had whistled after her and called out the most outrageous compliments to her—but then none of them had ever set eyes on Pearl!

Henry had taken her to a small *ristorante* in the village for lunch.

"I thought we were going to your place for lunch," she had said innocently.

"It would cause a deal of gossip," he had told her grimly.

"Let them gossip, I don't care!" she had declared.

"But Mario would," he had retorted. *"Meglio soli che male accompagnati!"*

"Meaning?" she had questioned him.

"That it is better to be alone than in bad company," he had translated. "Especially if you are a woman in Sicily," he had added meaningly.

Ruth had been tempted to ignore his warning, but a single look at Giulia's face on her return to the Verdecchio house had convinced her that Henry knew what he was talking about.

"Signor Verdecchio is not yet back," Giulia told her as she answered the door.

"Has his aunt come yet?" Ruth almost pleaded with her

Giulia shook her head. "She is not expected," she said flatly.

Ruth would have liked to have asked Henry to stay, but he wouldn't.

"You don't understand," he told her helplessly.

36

"You're Mario's girl, and that means something in these parts."

"But I'm not!" she denied hotly.

"Tell that to Mario!" he said.

It was very lonely after he had gone. Ruth watched the sun go down from the garden, the little dog playing about her feet. She was still there when Guilia called her in to supper.

"I don't think I ought to stay if he doesn't come soon," she told Giulia as the Italian woman served her with a bowl of soup.

"When you are finished I will take you to your room," Giulia answered, ignoring the English girl's doubts.

Ruth knew that the Italian woman disapproved of her, but she was too tired to care. Perhaps, she thought, it would be silly to leave the house now. Mario's aunt was sure to come sooner or later and then everything would be all right.

But when it came to it she was afraid to go to bed on her own in Mario's house. If he had been there that morning she would be back in Naples by now, braving Pearl's anger rather than his. But he had not been here and she would be poor-spirited indeed if she didn't tell him exactly what she thought of his treatment of her sister before she went!

The bedroom Giulia had prepared for her was large and rather beautiful. Thin, fragile carpets, woven into lovely patterns, covered most of the walls, and the four-poster bed delighted her. Giulia brought her a jug of hot water and dourly said good-night, her heavy footsteps dying away down the long passage to the stairs.

Ruth shut and locked the door on to the landing, wishing that she had thought to bring the dog up to her room with her. She wondered if Giulia would think her very odd if she went downstairs and collected him, and decided that she didn't care.

The dog was more than pleased to be invited into the house. He ran up the stairs ahead of her, his tail waving from side to side. She whistled to him to come into her room and laughed to herself as he sprang straight up on to the bed and curled up to go to sleep. She followed him into the bed, shivering slightly for the night was cool, and together they settled down to sleep until morning.

CHAPTER THREE

SOME time in the night the dog got off the bed and barked raucously. Ruth awoke and glanced about her. A slit of light shone into her room through a door she had not known was there.

"Here, dog!" she muttered.

The small animal jumped back on to the bed and licked her face, pleased to have got some response from somebody. The light went out and there was silence in the house. Ruth turned over and slept again.

Giulia's footsteps, stumping along the landing, awakened her. It was still very early. Ruth got out of bed and went to the window hoping to catch the last of the sunrise, but the sun was already too high and the honey-coloured land was bleached by its strong light, splashed here and there by the green of olive and citrus trees.

Giulia knocked on her door and came straight in with a cup of coffee in her hand.

"What is the dog doing here?" she asked dourly.

Ruth smiled at the small animal. "He kept me company," she defended him. "What's his name?"

"Saro." The Italian woman softened a little. "You had better let me take him back to the stables before the Signor sees him! Though he can hardly have helped to hear him in the night."

That reminded Ruth about the other door to her room. She looked round expecting to see it, but only the one out to the landing was visible.

"I thought I saw a light—" she said, puzzled.

"That'll be the door through to the Signor's room," Giulia told her, her black eyes fastened to Ruth's face. "I expect the Signor thought you were tired," she went on. "Look, it is here!"

Ruth watched fascinated as Giulia touched one of the doors of what she had taken to be a built-in wardrobe.

"I hope it's locked!" she observed. Giulia gave her a look that cast her into an immediate panic. "It is locked, isn't it?" she insisted.

"Signor Verdecchio has the key," Giulia sniffed. "These rooms were once used by his father." She pointed to the bed that Ruth had just vacated. "The Signor was born in that very bed! This was his mother's room when she was alive. No one has slept in here since."

"Then—then why—?"

Giulia sniffed again. "I obey orders," she answered.

She tried to pick up Saro to take him downstairs, but the dog ran under the bed yapping furiously.

"You'd better leave him," Ruth said.

"If you say so," Giulia shrugged. "The Signor does not allow his dogs in the house—"

"I will tell him that I brought him upstairs," Ruth answered with a great deal more confidence than she felt.

"I suppose it will be all right then," the Italian woman agreed. "I'll be in the kitchen when you want me."

Ruth was glad to see her go. She huddled back under the bedclothes and sipped her coffee in a dream, only it was more like a nightmare! She would have to face Mario, she thought dismally, though her courage for that seemed to have disappeared during the night. But she would tell him that she was going straight back to Naples and that so long as he didn't interfere with her sister again, he need never set eyes on her again.

But in fact she never had the opportunity to voice any of these fine sentiments. She had almost finished her coffee when the door in the wardrobe swung open, startling her so much that she spilled the remains of the coffee in the saucer and hastily put it down on the table beside her bed.

"At last, *cara*, I am here with you!"

The teasing, warm Italian voice reduced Ruth's courage to zero. She pulled the bedclothes closer about her and shut her eyes.

"Do you forgive me for not being here yesterday?" he went on. "I had to visit a friend who was dying. Happily, my aunt was there also and I was able to come away. And now, my darling—"

He advanced into the room and came face to face with Ruth's frightened gaze. "Miss Arnold!" he exclaimed. "What are you doing here?"

Ruth swallowed hard. "I might well ask you the same question!" she retorted warmly.

He was exactly as she had remembered him. The same cynical expression and the same ruthless look in his eyes. She shivered, for there was nothing kind about him. To her surprise an irrepressible smile crept into his eyes. He shrugged his shoulders, elegantly clad in a silk dressing gown, spreading his hands in an eloquent gesture.

"This is my house, Miss Arnold. I am accustomed to living here."

Ruth was forced to admit that there was a certain justice in that. She hugged Saro to her under the blankets and said forcefully: "But I am not accustomed to receiving men in my bedroom!"

She was grateful that he didn't laugh. Instead he looked at her for a long moment, taking in every detail of her face. She could feel herself blushing and wished that she had outgrown such a childish habit. Pearl *never* blushed, she remembered uneasily.

"I imagine not!" he said at last. It hardly sounded like a compliment.

"So," she said with a rush, "I would prefer to continue this conversation downstairs!" Her effect was somewhat ruined by Saro's wriggles. The dog's head slowly emerged out of the bedclothes, uttering a series of joyous yaps.

Mario was outraged. "Saro!"

The dog shook himself happily. He ran down to the bottom of the bed, tail waving, pleased to have Mario's attention riveted on himself.

"I asked him upstairs," Ruth explained hurriedly. "He—he didn't mind."

"I imagine not!" Mario said dryly. "He is also probably covered with fleas!"

"He is not!" Ruth protested indignantly.

"For your sake, I hope not!" he rejoined.

Ruth lifted her chin belligerently. "Anyway, if I'm prepared to risk it, I don't see what it has to do with you!"

Mario looked amused. "You are not very like your sister, are you?" he remarked.

Ruth eyed him crossly. "I have always found comparisons to be quite odious, besides being very bad manners!" she informed him.

His lips twitched. "Have you?"

"Yes, I have!" she agreed with vigour. "I can see for myself that Pearl has fantastic hair, that her eyes are a delicious blue, and that she is particularly well named! I don't have to have it pointed out to me—"

"Is that why you came instead?" Mario interrupted her, his face darkening.

Ruth was genuinely astonished. "No!" She could

tell at a glance that he didn't believe her. "You don't *understand*!" she said bitterly.

"Evidently not," he agreed lightly. "Perhaps you had better explain it to me?"

Ruth pleated the edge of the top sheet, unconsciously revealing her nervousness. "I'm afraid you are going to be very angry—" she began.

"Very likely!" Mario put in grimly.

"Well, it's all your own fault!" Ruth retorted with spirit. "I can't imagine why you thought Pearl would come in the first place!"

Mario frowned. "Do you mean that she connived at your taking her place?" he demanded.

Ruth's eyes fell. "Not exactly," she managed.

"I thought not," he rejoined. "I am not at all naïve, Miss Arnold. You will do far better to tell me the truth! The damage that your meddling has done unfortunately can't be undone, but this is not the moment for coy untruths!"

Ruth felt thoroughly frightened. "Pearl is not what you think her," she said hoarsely. "She may have given you the impression—"

Mario snorted contemptuously. The sheer haughtiness of his expression unnerved her sadly and only the thought of what would have happened if Pearl had come made her go on.

"Pearl is very young and—and not very wise. She—"

"My dear Miss Arnold—"

"I am not your dear anything!" she cut him off, thoroughly nettled.

"No? I am afraid we shall have to grow accustomed to one another sooner or later," he drawled.

Ruth sat up very straight. "I shall go back to Naples immediately," she decided. "If you're not going to listen—"

The amusement came back into his face. "I am all ears," he assured her. "You were telling me about your sister's virtues."

Ruth glared at him. "You are a great deal older than she is and I think she may have been carried away," she said with as much calmness as she could muster. She was quite unprepared for Mario's quick laughter. "She has always been very attractive to men," she continued with difficulty, "and she doesn't in the least realise the effect she is having on them."

"I am aware that your sister is young and silly!"

"I suppose that's why you thought—" Ruth hesitated. She forced herself to meet Mario's arrogant stare.

"Yes, Miss Arnold?" he prompted her.

"I suppose that's why you thought you could bring her here," she ended lamely.

"I invited her here at *her* request," he stated with so much conviction that Ruth was forced to believe him.

"She can't have understood!" Ruth insisted helplessly.

Mario smiled at her quite gently. "My dear, she is not the little innocent having a good time that you suppose. It is not my way to go round seducing innocent young women!"

Ruth put her hands up to her hot cheeks. "Pearl may have given you the wrong impression—"

"She was perfectly explicit from the very beginning!" Mario walked over to the window and stared moodily out of it. "If either of you are the innocents you would have me believe, I fear it is you, Miss Arnold!"

Ruth wondered if it could possibly be true. "I'll have you know that I have earned my own living for a matter of years!" she objected, trying not to cry.

He was unimpressed. "Where? In a convent?" he snorted.

"In a school," she admitted. "But it's far from being the cloistered kind of existence you seem to imagine it to be!"

He gave her a long, sober look. "I hope so," he said at last, "for your own sake!"

"I am very well able to look after myself!" she insisted bleakly.

"That I take leave to doubt! You could hardly have made a bigger mess of things if you had tried."

"I don't see why!" she retorted. "I shall go back to Naples by the quickest way possible and that will be that."

"That will not be that," he said dryly. "I told you that it isn't my habit to seduce innocent young women."

"But you haven't," she said, not without some satisfaction. "I saw to that!"

Mario's expression was one of a man sorely tried. "On the contrary," he told her, restraining himself with difficulty. "As far as the whole of Sicily is concerned, you are quite hopelessly compromised! Do you think they don't know that I paid for your ticket; that it was my car that met you at Palermo; and that it was my bed you slept in last night?"

Ruth gave Saro an agitated stroke behind his ears. "But you weren't in it," she reminded him weakly.

"Only because I was so late home," he answered with grim humour.

"But as soon as you knew I wasn't Pearl—"

He turned and looked at her. "You flatter me with a better nature than I actually have. Has no one ever told you, Miss Arnold, that in the dark all women look the same"

Ruth wished that she was half as sophisticated as

she had pretended to be. "What are you going to do?" she whispered.

"I have no choice. I shall marry you."

"Indeed you won't!" Ruth said shortly. "I don't know how you can even think of such a thing!" she added with strong disapproval. "You weren't thinking of marrying Pearl, were you?"

She looked so anxious that Mario relented towards her. "We are not considering Pearl for the moment, we are considering you," he said, not without humour.

Ruth lifted her chin with unconscious dignity. "Pearl and I are sisters," she said firmly.

"If you weren't, I shouldn't hesitate to tell you that Pearl hasn't a moral to her name! Not that you appear to have many—reading other people's letters! Stealing travel tickets! And even now you haven't the remotest idea of what you've done!"

Ruth blinked. "I may be stupid, but at least I meant well!"

"Spare me your good intentions!" Mario stormed at her. "It is well known which roads are paved with them!"

Ruth bit her lip. An irrepressible urge to giggle defeated her. "I always knew Pluto lived about these parts," she said. "Are you he, by any chance?"

Mario looked impossibly angry. "Are you joking?"

The desire to giggle left her. "I'm sorry," she said.

"Anyway, what do you know about Roman legends?" he said crossly. "That story was born in Sicily. Did you know that?"

Ruth nodded solemnly. "Do you think the under-world was the same place as Hell?" she asked him.

"No, I do not. Nor am I any relation to Hell's guardian, whatever you might think! Am I really so impossible?"

She cast him a shy look. To tell the truth she didn't find him impossible at all. She was a little frightened of him, she thought, particularly when he glared at her down his long nose, but she could quite easily grow used to that. He was, she discovered with some surprise, a great deal nicer than she had supposed.

"No," she said in a stifled voice, "I don't find you impossible."

"Nor I you. In fact I am becoming more reconciled by the minute to our marriage—"

"Don't be silly!" she reproved him.

He sat on the end of her bed, a slight smile on his face. "I wish it could be as easily resolved as you think," he sighed. "But this is Sicily, my dear, not the green fields of England. There's not a soul who won't believe that we spent the night together and, in Sicily, there is only one conclusion that can come of that. I must marry you as soon as possible!"

"But I'm going back to England. I don't care if they do doubt my honour!" Ruth said heatedly.

"It is *my* honour which is in question," he replied.

"But why should you *care*?" she wondered.

"Perhaps because I do live in Sicily. If your advent had been a little less public, we might have put a good face on it. But Giulia has already spoken to her family and so on. Nor," he added wryly, "do I suppose that you had the good sense to stay close to the house all day yesterday?" One glance at her face told him that she had not. "What did you do?" he asked her.

"Henry Brett took me to see the new scheme," she confessed humbly.

"So the whole village saw you!" he groaned.

"They saw us both," she admitted. "We had lunch in the little restaurant there."

He groaned. "And watched you come back here, I suppose?"

She was silent. She was wise enough to know that she had very little understanding of the Sicilian code of behaviour. Wryly, she remembered how she had warned Pearl about their peculiar ideas of honour that forced any compromised girl into marriage whether she wished it or not. She had never even remotely suspected that it might happen to her!

"That isn't all," she blurted out finally. "On the boat, I shared a cabin with your aunt, and I told her all about it!"

"You did what?" The menace in his voice was unmistakable.

Ruth's hand went up to her mouth. "You shouldn't have addressed your letter to Miss Arnold," she countered. "You must have known that I am the elder sister!"

"A nice point!" he said nastily. "I wondered what excuse you had for reading your sister's letter."

"Her name wasn't even mentioned!"

Mario laughed without any humour at all. "And so you supposed that I was writing to you? On a few minutes' acquaintance?"

"No, I didn't," Ruth admitted. "But I had to do something! I knew you were out to hurt Pearl, and now that you can't, you're going to hurt me instead!" She tried valiantly not to cry, failed, and wiped the tears angrily from her cheeks. "Well, you won't!" she tossed at him. "I don't care—that!—for your honour, so there!" She flicked her fingers at him, more than ever annoyed by his laughter.

"Truly, my love, I shall not hurt you," he promised her. "But if my aunt knows of your visit here she will have lost no time in telling my mother. If you had any choice in the matter, I am afraid

48

that you now have none at all! Marry me you will, and soon!"

Ruth knew that she should have felt nothing but misery at the thought, but a curious sense of elation fountained up within her. She had felt at home from the instant she had set foot on Sicilian soil and the prospect of never having to leave the island again could not help appealing to her.

"But I can't do that to Pearl!" she exclaimed. "For, whatever you say about her, if you think you have to marry me, you would have felt the same about her!"

Mario's face fell into its familiar, cynical lines. "I think not," he said. "No one could possibly imagine that I was the first man Pearl had ever known—"

"But that's barbaric!" Ruth exclaimed, shocked.

His smile mocked her. "It is Sicilian!"

"Besides being unkind," Ruth added painfully. "I don't think you're right about Pearl. And even if you are, I don't think it's very chivalrous to say so!"

He said nothing, only smiled with real amusement.

"*And*," Ruth went on, her sense of grievance getting the better of her, "I may not be as pretty as my sister, but I have had *some* boy-friends of my own!"

He was unfeeling enough to laugh aloud. He reached forward and took her face in his hand, forcing her to look at him.

"No, you're not as pretty as Pearl!"

Ruth blushed. "You're hurting me!" she complained.

"I am not!" he retorted. "Don't lie to me, Ruth! And if you really want to know, you're not pretty at all! But you have the rudiments of beauty. You ought to accentuate your eyes when you make up and do something about your hair. I'll see that you do when you're my wife!"

"Then the occasion will never arise!" Ruth said somewhat smugly.

His eyes lit. "Is that a challenge?" He came closer still and kissed her gently on the lips. "I never refuse a challenge. Remember that!"

She was sadly shaken. She watched in a fright as he slowly rose to his feet. He was so very tall and his broken nose gave him a devilish look that scared her.

"N-nor do I!" she stammered bravely.

"Indeed?" She wished he didn't look quite as though he were enjoying himself so much. "Then I'll make the necessary arrangements as soon as possible."

He was gone before she could think up a sufficiently stinging retort, shutting the communicating door with a sharp click. Her bravery fell away from her and she felt cold and shivery. It was a pretty pickle! She wondered what they would have said in the staff room of the school where she taught, but her imagination failed her. There they had all the correct, liberal ideas of how people ought to behave. They were more likely to discuss the price of food than the archaic customs of a foreign people, with quaint ideas of a woman's honour and shotgun weddings!

But there was one thing that disturbed her more than anything else. Despite her fear of him, even her disapproval of him, she found that she *liked* Mario Verdecchio. She liked his strange humour and the strength in his fingers when he touched her. He was unexpected, and being with him was like a ride on a scenic railway, as exhilarating as it was frightening. Of course it was ridiculous to consider, even for a minute, that she would marry him, but she couldn't help thinking that life was going to be very tame back in England, in the school where she taught, when he wouldn't be there to taunt her.

Saro went to the door and whined gently, looking sorrowfully over his shoulder at her.

"I'm coming," she told him.

There was one thing about a dog, he gave one something to do. Ruth dressed quickly and went downstairs with him into the rough garden at the side of the house. There was a path that went steeply uphill and through a clump of cypress trees. Saro went first, his tail held aloft, sniffing every inch of the path as he went along to see who had been there since the day before. Ruth followed at a more leisurely pace, looking back at the house at intervals, admiring the classical lines of the house behind her.

She was surprised, when she arrived at the cypress trees, to find herself overlooking the sea. The cliff fell away beneath her, honeycombed with the holes that birds had used for nesting earlier in the summer. Beneath was the deep blue of the sea, edged with white as it broke against the rocks beneath. In a nearby vineyard a man was singing a Neapolitan love song, such as she had heard from her very youth. She smiled to herself with sheer enjoyment, remembering a story that she had once been told about Sicily. The angel Gabriel had been astonished by the beauty of the island. 'What are you going to do?' he had asked God. 'The island is so desirable that everyone will fight over it.' 'I shall fill it with Sicilians,' God had answered.

The scene was so beautiful that Ruth stopped for a while to look the longer. A fallen tree served as a more than adequate seat and Saro, who had apparently adopted her as a more or less permanent companion, ran in and out of the trees, returning to her at intervals for a few words of admiration and approval.

Henry Brett had found her name apt the day before, she remembered. But she had no desire to weep. She was not in the least homesick. But there was, she thought, something in the poem that struck a chord. She began to recite it softly to herself, to see what it sounded like, away from the classroom, in surroundings that were made for such cadences.

Thou wast not born for death, immortal Bird!
No hungry generations tread thee down;
The voice I hear this passing night was heard
In ancient days by emperor and clown!
Perhaps the self-same song that found a path
Through the sad heart of Ruth, when, sick for home,
She stood in tears amid the alien corn;
The same that oft times hath
Charmed magic casements, opening on the foam
Of perilous seas, in faery lands forlorn.

There was no nightingale, not at that hour of the morning, and Ruth couldn't honestly say that she felt in the least bit alien, but the magic casements were there before her, and the perilous seas she could feel in her very blood. Perhaps the choice was apter than Henry Brett had known.

She turned as she heard hurrying footsteps coming up the path and went to meet Giulia, cross and panting, as she came towards her.

"The Signor is angry because you have not had breakfast!" the Italian woman said furiously. "In England you would have eaten egg and bacon—many things—and he says you must have the same here!"

Ruth blinked. "But I never eat breakfast!" she objected.

"Then you had better tell Signor Verdecchio so yourself!" Giulia insisted grimly.

Ruth chuckled. "I'm afraid I'm being a great nuisance to you," she apologised.

Giulia gave her a sudden smile. "It is no trouble for me, but," she added with a shake of her head, "it is trouble for you! The Signor's aunt will be with

52

us for lunch, now that her friend has died. She will not expect to find you here."

But she would, Ruth thought. She knew all about her! And when she came, she would sort out the whole situation and Ruth would go back to England.

But she couldn't help wondering why the thought gave her so little pleasure.

CHAPTER FOUR

RUTH succeeded in avoiding Mario all day. Signora Verdecchio had not turned up at lunchtime after all. Ruth had looked for her arrival, but no car had come up the drive to the house and Giulia had resignedly shrugged her shoulders and declared that it was always the same, the Signora had no idea of time, that she scarcely knew that the sun came up in the morning and went down at night.

At five o'clock in the afternoon, she did finally arrive. Ruth could just catch a glimpse of the front door from her bedroom window and she had watched Mario stride out of the door to take her luggage, saluting his vivacious aunt on either cheek. The Signora, Ruth was surprised to see, was clothed entirely in black and looked rather older than she had remembered her. Then she remembered it had been a friend of hers who had died and that she was probably already in mourning.

It was the beginning of an exhausting evening. Lucia Verdecchio had come originally from a local family before she had married Mario's father's younger brother. She knew everyone for miles around and, hearing that she was there, mourning her dead friend, it seemed to Ruth that the whole island came to pay their respects to her. A never-ending stream of people passed in and out of the house, looking around with curious eyes. If Ruth had been in any doubt before, she knew now that everyone had already heard all about her. With secret eyes, veiling their thoughts, they congratulated Mario on his good fortune.

But it was only at dinner, when the people had gone, that Signora Verdecchio had time to give her nephew's affairs her full attention.

"When is the priest coming?" she asked Mario.

He looked at her with real affection. "I had arranged for him to come today, but we thought we'd wait for you to grace the occasion with your presence."

"Very proper!" his aunt commented.

"But," Ruth began, "now that your aunt is here, surely there is no need—"

Signora Verdecchio gave her a long, hard look. "You had better take Italian lessons in Palermo," she directed, just as if Ruth hadn't spoken at all.

"Well, I won't!" Ruth said sulkily.

"And you will need some clothes—"

"And she needs to have her hair fixed!" Mario put in.

His aunt nodded. "I will take her in the morning to a little place I know," she said comfortably. "You had better arrange with the priest to come at midday."

"I won't be married to anyone!" Ruth said loudly.

Mario smiled straight into her eyes. "You won't find it so dreadful," he told her. "I'll see to that!"

"But that isn't the point!" Ruth exclaimed.

"No," Lucia Verdecchio agreed sagely, "that is not the point. The point is that the whole family has been wanting Mario to marry for a long time, and now he is going to. I have already told his mother all about it. A nice girl, I said. A *very* nice girl! Not quite in Mario's usual circle, but that is a good thing, no doubt. We are all very pleased!"

Ruth stared at her. "I don't believe you!" she said faintly. "I thought you would *help* me!"

Lucia Verdecchio nodded complacently. "But that is what I am doing! There is nothing for it but for you to marry Mario, and I intend to stay on here and then everyone will see that the family approves. It would have been different, perhaps, if I had been here at the house last night, but—" She shrugged elegantly.

"Where were you last night?" Ruth asked, suddenly extremely angry, angry with the Verdecchios, and still more angry with herself for getting into such a silly position.

Mario's aunt looked innocent. "Were you hoping I would look in? But how could I leave the deathbed of my friend?"

"You appear to have had a nice conversation with my mother," Mario reminded her dryly.

"On the telephone," Lucia Verdecchio nodded. "She sounded as though she were in the next room! And to think she is in New York! It was my duty to set her mind at rest," she went on virtuously. "She had heard—many things that were not to her taste at all! How could I not tell her about our dear Ruth?"

Mario gave her a sardonic look. "And how did she know about these—many things?"

"I have really no idea!" his aunt replied. "As you know, I live quietly in Tunis. I have no knowledge of what you do or don't do! But the Verdecchios are well known all over southern Italy. What do you expect. That your friends will suddenly give up the natural pleasure of having a good gossip? *Mamma mia*, you expect a great deal!"

"Well, *I* am not known all over southern Italy," Ruth objected. "I shall go back to Naples tomorrow, and Pearl and I will go straight back to England! So you needn't worry about us at all."

"You will do as you're told!" Mario growled at her.

Ruth lifted her chin. "By whom?"

"By your husband!" he snapped.

"But you're not my husband," she returned sweetly.

"In Sicily," he warned her with careful enunciation, "women are better seen and not heard!"

"And I'm not Sicilian either!" Ruth informed him loftily. "If you want to know, I am very glad I am English. *And* I believe in equality between the sexes!"

Signora Verdecchio smiled pacifically. "Of course you do!" She took a quick sip of wine. "I do myself!"

"Then how—?" Ruth began.

Mario choked. "I never thought to hear you say it, aunt," he drawled.

"But it is so!" that lady insisted. "I assure you. All women think so—that is only natural! Only, from one place to another we go about it in different ways. In England you make a great noise; you demonstrate; and you wear your hair shorter than the men. In Sicily, we do none of those things. Here, it is the family that matters. The woman *is* the family! It is quite obvious, is it not? It is necessary for the man to marry a nice girl who will be the mother of his sons. It is so easy for a man not to be the father, but with the *mother*, it is apparent, no?"

"Quite apparent," Ruth was forced to agree.

"So we protect our women and, therefore, our families!" Signora Verdecchio concluded in triumph. "It is not quite equal, perhaps, but the men feel they are equal and so all is well."

This was not an argument that had previously occurred to Ruth. She was sure that there was a flaw in it somewhere, especially when it came to how it affected her personally, but for the moment it sounded almost reasonable.

"I still won't marry Mario," she said clearly. "I'll tell the priest as much! He can hardly force me into marriage."

Mario smiled faintly. "*Il padre* is a little deaf."

57

"Then I'll shout!" she retorted.

"I think not," he answered charmingly. "We are all equal, but some of us are a little more equal than others, like Mr. Orwell's pigs, was it not?"

"In fact you'll make me?" she challenged him.

He shrugged his shoulders, still smiling. "I hope it will not come to that," he said in disapproving tones.

"But why?" she demanded, tears stinging her eyes. "You *can't* want to marry me?"

He laughed shortly. "Perhaps not. But I know better than to fly in the face of destiny, my dear. And so, tomorrow, my wife you shall be!"

Ruth rose to her feet, leaving the meat course of her meal untasted. "I am going up to bed," she announced.

Mario politely rose as well. "Sleep well, *cara mia*," he said gently.

She turned at the doorway and glared at him. "And I'll thank you to lock the door between our rooms!" she said defiantly.

He looked amused. "You will not be disturbed—tonight," he promised her.

"I should think not!" his aunt bridled. "Am I not here to chaperone you?"

Ruth was in two minds about telling her that her promised chaperonage of the night before had hardly been effective, but she held her tongue. She would, she thought, need Mario's aunt for an ally when she made her escape to Naples.

"Shall I bring you a warm drink to your bed?" Giulia asked her as she went through the kitchen.

Ruth shook her head, thanking her warmly. "I only came for Saro," she said.

Giulia frowned. "The Signor will have other ideas after tonight!" she said with heavy humour.

Ruth blushed. "We'll see," she said with a dour

dignity that seemed to be all that was left to her. And she scuttled off to bed, with the little dog dancing along at her heels, pleased and excited by the prospect of another night inside the house.

Lucia Verdecchio drove Ruth into Palermo herself.

"I have discussed it with Mario and we have decided exactly how you must wear your hair," she explained as they made a rather erratic start down the long drive.

Ruth looked at her soberly. "It's very kind of you," she said hesitantly, "but I'm going back to Naples. Pearl will be frantic with worry by now! It would be very kind of you, if you'll take me to the boat."

Signora Verdecchio pushed the car into top gear and frowned. "There is no boat today from Palermo. Now really, you mustn't worry, my dear! You'll feel better when you've had your hair done!"

Ruth relapsed into silence. She was being railroaded with a vengeance! But she wouldn't have it! Sooner or later, some time during the morning, she would escape the custody of Mario's aunt. There must be some way of getting off this island, and she would find it if it was the last thing she did!

Meanwhile, there was a certain excitement about going to a top-class hairdresser. She had never been able to afford such luxuries on her salary at home.

"Luigi is very clever!" Signora Verdecchio told her, here whole being glowing with enthusiasm. "We must have you looking your best for your wedding, musn't we?"

Ruth nodded, for it was quite useless to argue with the older woman.

"Tell me about Mario's mother," she suggested instead.

Signora Verdecchio was inordinately pleased at this

sign of interest in The Family. She gave Ruth a look of such complete approval that Ruth felt guilty. She was interested in Mario's mother, but not at all as her future mother-in-law.

"Why is she in New York?" she asked.

Signora Verdecchio was surprised. "She lives there!"

"In New York?" Ruth exclaimed.

Signora Verdecchio apparently thought that this interesting fact did need some kind of explanation. "She married the elder brother and I the younger," she said. "Her husband died a few years ago and she couldn't stand living in Sicily with all the family dispersed. At that time, Mario was in Milan looking round for suitable small industries that he could bring to Sicily, and my husband and I were living in Tunis. She was dull by herself—"

"But what about her family?" Ruth objected.

Lucia Verdecchio looked very well satisfied with herself. "That's why she went to New York," she said slyly. "Mary-Anne is an American."

"And was she kidnapped too?" Ruth asked dryly.

"She was very much in love with her husband!" Lucia retorted. "And with Sicily too. The family— especially her son—means a great deal to her."

She sounded an odd kind of person to Ruth. What woman in her right mind would have tied herself down to this narrow, old-fashioned island, when she had been born an American?

"Her husband must have been very different from Mario!" she observed.

"In what way?" the Signora asked, laughing.

"Mario expects a woman to have no views of her own at all!" Ruth burst out. "I'm sure he wants a wife who will keep the house running smoothly, and bring up his children, and do *exactly* what he says—"

The Signora laughed. "My dear, Mario is modern

compared to his father! Now he was an autocrat of the old order. But Mary-Anne wouldn't have had him any different. Her freedom, since his death, hasn't brought her any happiness."

"Well, I don't intend to put myself in the position of being a doormat to any man!" Ruth said briskly.

Signora Verdecchio laughed again. "You are so exactly right for Mario!" she exclaimed.

Ruth was startled into an uncomfortable silence, that was only broken by their arrival in Palermo at the hairdressers. Signora Verdecchio parked the car with a gay abandon as to the parking rules and allowed herself to be bowed into the *salon* with all the charm and dignity that Ruth was beginning to associate with all the Verdecchios.

"I want you to meet my niece," she said in cool, clear Italian so that even Ruth could understand her. "Today she gets married and, as you can see, her hair-style is not in the fashion. I think a good cut, no? A manicure? And it is necessary for her to have make-up to improve her face!"

"At once, *signora*! If the *signorina* will pass this way—?"

Ruth was led away into a perfumed cubicle while chattering Italians hurried back and forth, turning Signora Verdecchio's vague instructions into reality. A pretty young girl shampooed her hair, marvelling at Ruth's good fortune in getting married that very day. And to Mario Verdecchio! There was no man who had been more sought after! He was rich, good-looking, and doing all that he could to improve the local conditions of his people! How flattered Ruth must feel! How she must die at the very thought of being loved by such a man!

Ruth assured her that she was managing to bear up, though she had to admit to herself that she did

61

feel weak inside if she allowed herself to dwell on the thought of Mario as her husband. Not that he was going to be! But she felt a definite sinking feeling when she thought of his relief when he discovered that she had escaped him.

By the time the master hairdresser himself came into her cubicle she was decidedly depressed. She was as plain as she had ever looked, with her hair dripping around her shoulders and her face innocent even of the modicum of make-up that she customarily wore.

"Mmm. You must look beautiful," the tall, elegant man said thoughtfully. "It is not easy. No, not easy at all!"

Ruth's self-confidence took another dive. The man pulled her wet hair over her eyes and back again.

"I like my hair the way it is," Ruth said crossly.

But the man paid no attention to her. "Ah yes! I have it!" he exclaimed. "Now we shall cut it!"

In a flash he had produced his razor out of his pocket and had taken a wild slash at a lock of her hair. Ruth winced, not daring to look at what he was doing. She had to admit that he was quick, though. In a few seconds most of her hair was lying in piles around her chair.

"Isn't that short enough?" she asked him timidly.

"It is not so short," he cajoled her. "It is to give it shape. It has enough curl to make it easy to keep and that is necessary for someone who takes so little trouble. If you have the shape, you have everything!"

He clapped his hands and yet another assistant brought a trolley full of curlers and pins. His fingers flew over Ruth's head and the style he had chosen for her began to take shape.

"We will have the manicure under the drier," he told her softly. "The artist who does the make-up will

62

come along later, when we have finished with your hair and you can see the results better. You have something to read?" He handed her a couple of copies of *Oggi* and departed, leaving her to her lonely thoughts.

It was difficult, though, not to be excited when she saw the final results. Her hair formed a soft frame to her face in a way that did not lessen the character of her face, but somehow made her look more feminine and gave her personality a warmth. It had always been there, she knew, but she had suppressed any ideas she might have had in that direction so that she would look older in the classroom. Now, looking at herself in the glass, she couldn't help being pleased with the transformation he had achieved.

"It's just as well I'm not teaching anyone anything this afternoon!" she remarked with wry amusement to Signora Verdecchio who had come to inspect the result.

"It is a step!" the other lady congratulated herself. "We have you—almost beautiful, and you see, already you are less stern! Soon you will feel quite gay that you are a woman!"

She beckoned to the middle-aged woman who was to teach Ruth how to put on her make-up and the two of them went into a huddle together, deciding which of Ruth's features should be brought into prominence, and which rigidly suppressed. But about this, Ruth suddenly discovered she had very definite ideas of her own.

"I have quite nice eyes," she said bravely.

"Indeed!" they all agreed in an admiring chorus.

"Well then, I'd like to make them more obvious," she went on.

The make-up artist nodded in complete agreement. "Someone has told you this, yes?" she teased her customer gently. "He is quite right! In two moments you will see it for yourself!"

Ruth remembered with a blush that it had been none other than Mario who had remarked about her eyes. She began to wish that she had said nothing, but had left it all to Signora Verdecchio She had no ambition to make herself pleasing to Mario! Or had she? The sudden doubt as to her own motives unnerved her.

The Italian lady was definite. She set out her tray of cosmetics with deft fingers, explaining simply the purpose of each item as she laid it down.

"Now, any questions?" she said at the end of her dissertation.

Ruth looked at the selection in horror. "But I can't put on all that!" she objected.

"No, no, not all of it. Some eyelashes, I think, though, you must have!"

Ruth was surprised to discover how easy they were to apply. Once her unaccustomed fingers had mastered the art, she could put them on in a matter of seconds and they looked quite natural. It was the same with the eye make-up that her mentor insisted on her using.

"Before you look," the lady said at last, "we will have a touch of rouge on the cheeks and a quite pale lipstick. There! Now you may look!"

Ruth stared at herself for a long moment. She was not almost beautiful any longer. She *was* beautiful. And she wasn't the only person who thought so. She could tell by the sudden silence amongst the group that had gone to work on her. Looking at herself, she felt that the difference between beauty and mere prettiness had been drawn pretty clearly. She was very glad that Pearl was not there to see this transformation, for Pearl wasn't used to being second to her sister.

"I look nice, don't you think?" she said hesitantly to Lucia Verdecchio.

"It is just as Mario said it would be!" that lady claimed firmly. "You are quite lovely, my dear!"

Ruth blushed at the mention of Mario's name. She could scarcely tear her eyes away from her reflection in the glass. It was as though she were looking at a stranger, with whom she had something in common, but not very much. This stranger, this beautiful stranger, had a vulnerable look that Ruth had never detected in herself.

"Mario will be pleased!" his aunt was saying.

"I didn't do it for Mario!" Ruth retorted.

Their laughter told her that nobody there believed her, not even Signora Verdecchio. Ruth watched her as she paid the extremely large bill without a blink, showering her approval on everyone in the *salon*.

"My niece will be coming here regularly from now on," she told them happily. "I can promise you that! You will look after her, won't you? I can't stay in Sicily for long this time. My husband needs me in Tunis."

They promised that Ruth would always receive the very best attention from them whether the Signora was there or not. The tips were large enough to encourage the proprietor to escort Signora Verdecchio and Ruth right to the car.

"It is always a pleasure to serve any of the Verdecchios," he bowed.

Lucia glowed with content. "It has been very successful!" she smiled. "I am very well pleased!"

She glanced at her watch as soon as they were alone. "It is eleven already. That allows us half an hour to get ready for the ceremony if we go home now—"

Ruth gave her a desperate look. "Signora, we can't go back immediately," she pleaded. "I can't! Besides," she added, "I haven't any of my things with me—"

"I have seen to all that," Lucia Verdecchio assured her. "You have no need to worry."

"I haven't even got a present for Mario," Ruth put in guiltily. She felt awful saying such a thing when she knew quite well that she would never give Mario *anything*. But she couldn't allow herself to be driven meekly back to Mario's house either. She had to go back to Naples—and to Pearl.

The Signora's eyebrows rose. "Do you want to give him something?" she asked in a deliberately neutral voice.

Ruth felt the burning colour leap to her cheeks. "It's—it's customary," she mumbled.

The Signora came close to grinning. "What a good idea! What did you have in mind?"

Ruth cast about in her mind, feeling more and more miserable by the minute. "I don't know," she said at last.

"A gold pen?" Lucia suggested. "You must forgive me for asking, but have you much money with you?"

"Enough for that," Ruth grunted. "Could we go somewhere more central and have a look at some?"

The Signora was only too glad to fall in with such a plan. Ruth felt like a traitor. If only the older woman didn't look quite so much like the cat who had swallowed the canary! If only she could bring herself to dislike her! And if only, oh yes, if only she could bring herself to dislike Mario instead of feeling weak in the stomach every time she thought of him!

"I saw a shop near the harbour," Ruth made herself say just as if she had only just thought of it.

"That's where we go!" the Signora agreed eagerly. "Wherever you say!"

She thrust the car through the narrow streets with determination. The pedestrians flattened themselves against the walls as they passed and a stall of melons collapsed under the sheer pressure of people. Some ragged children rushed down the street, the stolen melons in their hands. The stall-holder ran after them, puffing and fuming in the heat. He shook his fist at Signora Verdecchio and, looking a trifle dismayed, she came to a stop.

"The streets are too narrow—" she began to explain.

"Then drive your car somewhere else!" he advised her, his pudgy flesh trembling with anger.

"I'll help you pick the melons up," Ruth offered eagerly in her broken Italian.

A smile spread over his face as he recognised a foreigner. "Then you do accept full liability?" he demanded.

Signora Verdecchio stepped out of the car, a non-stop spurt of Italian issuing from her. Ruth would have loved to have stayed to hear the end of the incident, but she knew that she wouldn't get a better chance. If she were to escape, this was her opportunity.

She ran as hard as she could and found herself in the Piazza Kalsa, a fine square behind the Porta dei Greca, with its densely populated alleys, full of sailors and fishermen whose wives are famous for their lace-making and embroidery. The Kalsa is the most typically Arab part of the city and there were delightful little courts that Ruth would have loved to explore. As it was, she ran hither and thither, looking for the way to the port, but there seemed to be no end to the narrow alleys, most of them leading nowhere, or only back where she had been before.

Women, dressed all in black, and small, ragged boys watched her pass. She tried to ask them the way, but they only shook their heads and stared at her with black, apparently sightless eyes. She began to grow frightened and more and more desperate. And then suddenly there she was in the road that led to the port, although she had no idea of how she had got there.

Looking at her watch, she saw that it was already twenty to twelve. She tried to tell herself that it no longer mattered to her. Now that she was not going to be married at noon, the hour of twelve no longer held any meaning. She was cross with herself, therefore, for feeling bereft and forlorn by the knowledge. She sniffed hard and pressed on down the street. She would get on the first boat for Naples and that would be that!

The heat pressed down on her, but she refused to go any slower. She was almost sure that the ticket offices would close at twelve, for the long lunch hour that is universal all round the Mediterranean. She thought that she had made it when she was grasped tightly by the arm.

"I think not," Mario drawled in her ear.

She turned and faced him, hot and extremely angry. "But why not?" she pleaded. "You know you don't really want to marry me!"

His eyes widened as he took in her new hair-style and make-up. He whistled softly. It should, Ruth thought, have been humiliating to her to have anyone look at her like that, but it was not. If she were honest, she had to admit that it was pure balm to her shattered nerves.

"I—I *can't* marry you," she said.

He smiled. "I think you have no choice," he answered gently.

"But I won't—I *won't* marry you!"

He forced her to look up at him. His own eyes were alight with laughter and she could feel an answering quirk of sheer amusement and relief somewhere deep inside her.

"No?" he mocked her.

"No," she repeated in a shaken voice.

He shrugged. "It's a pity, don't you think, with all the preparations already made?" He touched her hair lightly with his fingers. "Was all this for yourself?" He bent and kissed her on the lips. "I think not," he said.

Ruth said nothing. She knew that if she had, it would have been a total surrender.

CHAPTER FIVE

THE wedding was hardly delayed at all. Mario had done no more than glance at his watch before he had rushed her back down the street to where Henry Brett was waiting with his jeep.

"Will you drive us back to the house?" Mario had asked him with all the charm he had at his command.

"What about your aunt?" Ruth had reminded him. "I left her somewhere over there," she added vaguely, not really sure which way she had come.

"She will know that I have you safe," Mario had said.

Ruth had been grateful for the unspoken sympathy of Henry Brett during the silent ride back to the house. It was only when they had arrived and the two of them were standing in the hall while Mario went to discover if the priest had arrived that Henry said:

"I gather the corn has been particularly alien this morning?"

Ruth shook her head. "It's so ridiculous!" she exclaimed helplessly.

Henry looked concerned. "I'd like to help—" he began.

"No, don't!" Ruth said quickly. "You'll lose your job, or—or something!"

Henry's mouth twisted into a rueful grin. "I very nearly did already," he admitted. "Your future lord and master was furious that I'd taken you round the village on your own. If I hadn't known that he didn't care a button for you, I'd have thought him the original jealous lover seeking revenge!"

Ruth went white. "I wish I could understand it all better," she sighed.

"I'd have thought Mario was easily understood," Henry remarked dryly. "He hates to be thwarted. It's as simple as that!"

"I don't think it can be," Ruth objected. "*Nobody* in Sicily seems to find it the least bit odd that *today* his wretched honour makes him have to marry me to save my honour!"

Henry grinned. "It does sound a bit medieval, put like that," he admitted.

"A bit!" she retorted. "*And* as far as I can see the damage to my honour is only a bit of possible local gossip! Can you beat that?"

"No," he reproved her, "that isn't quite fair. If you were a Sicilian girl, you wouldn't be able to make a respectable marriage after spending the night here. After all, he was here too!"

Ruth stared at him in disbelief. "But nothing *happened*!"

Henry's cheeks went a peculiar shade of pink. "I believe that, of course," he said awkwardly. "I mean, I believe it because you say so. I mean, Sicilians have pretty hot blood, don't they? You know, any opportunity and all that—"

"*Henry*!"

"Beg your pardon," he muttered unhappily.

"I should think so!" she said indignantly.

The colour was still in her cheeks and the light of battle in her eye when Signora Verdecchio came through the front door.

"Ah, there you are!" she said to Ruth. "You're a very naughty girl! I suppose Mario brought you back?"

Ruth nodded silently.

"He was right! He said you'd make for the port if you could." Her voice rose in anguish. "And I thought

71

you were persuaded that we were doing the best thing!"
she complained. "*And* you've messed up your hair!"

Ruth's hand went involuntarily to her hair, patting a
loose curl back into place. "I had to," she tried to
explain. "Mario and I don't want to marry one
another!"

"I won't believe that's true," the Signora fussed.
"Come here and I'll fix your hair!"

Ruth refused to feel guilty. Why should she? But
nevertheless she found herself hoping that Mario's aunt
was not too cross with her.

"It's so ridiculous!" she said aloud. "I can't believe
you are all serious about it even now!"

Lucia clicked her tongue against her teeth. "It is you
who are ridiculous!" she claimed fiercely. "Why, any
girl would be pleased to marry Mario! You will have
comfort and security and the joy of having a family
about you. What more do you want?"

"Love," Ruth said flatly.

To her astonishment, Signora Verdecchio laughed.
"And do you think that you won't fall in love with
Mario?" she demanded.

Ruth swallowed. "But will he fall in love with me?"

The Signora shrugged. "There are other things," she
told her. "This romantic love that you think so much
about is here today and gone tomorrow. You will have
respect as Mario's wife, and affection, and honour as the
mother of his children."

"But not love?" Ruth said sadly.

"It will come," Lucia said gently. "If you want it, it
will come."

But Ruth could not believe her. She allowed herself to
be pushed into the *salotto* and stood disconsolately in
the middle of the room, trying not to look at the
painting of the Verdecchio who was so like Mario.
There were flowers everywhere. It was a mockery, Ruth

thought, trying to give a festive air to what had to be an empty feast. Mario's aunt handed her a bouquet of white flowers that smelt heavily of orange blossom, and then Mario arrived with the priest.

She wondered what would happen if she told him that she was being married against her will, but she found herself smiling when he approached her.

"I don't speak English," the priest said apologetically. His thick Sicilian accent made his Italian almost unintelligible to Ruth as well. "It is a very happy occasion." He looked tired and defeated and went on to mutter something about not holding the wedding in church. Ruth came to the conclusion that it was because she was English and a stranger.

"He doesn't want to marry me!" she said in a burst, half in English and half in Italian, which the priest quite clearly didn't begin to understand. The old man nodded gently. "It is the custom," he said, as if he were agreeing with her.

"*Non parlo bene italiano*—" Ruth began desperately. She was aware of Mario coming towards her. In another moment, she knew, it would be too late!

"My love," he said, "are you ready for the ceremony?" He threaded his fingers through hers and squeezed her hand until it hurt.

"But—"

"But?" he echoed.

She was cast into instant confusion. He had called her *my love*! She tried to free her hand, but she could not. He stood quietly beside her, his Satanic looks becoming magnified in her mind, and making no effort at all to help her.

"Well, my love?" he repeated.

"I'm ready," she said.

He gave her a ring that had been in the Verdecchio

family since the time of Frederick II. He gave her gold in the form of a key to his house. And he gave her a silver coin as a symbol of his wealth.

To Ruth, the whole ceremony was as unreal as a dream. The priest mumbled and she couldn't really understand what he was saying. If Mario's responses were clear, her own were bungled as she struggled with the unfamiliar Italian formula that committed her life into Mario's keeping. Only when she was asked if she would take Mario to be her husband, to love him, to honour him, and to obey him, did she make a single, firm response. "*Si*," she said with a willingness that shocked her.

Mario glanced at her, his eyes full of swift amusement, and she could feel herself blushing in the most humiliating way. Then the moment passed and the instant of intimate understanding had gone with it. The priest mumbled on to a conclusion and the ceremony was over.

The civil part of the wedding was no more than a formality. Ruth signed half a dozen pieces of paper, wherever anyone told her she should, and received in return a document, heavy with seals, that she supposed was her marriage lines.

"Was it so painful?" Mario asked her mildly.

She didn't know how to answer. "I don't see how you can look so happy about it!" she retorted.

He smiled. "Don't you? There are compensations, you know."

"They're not obvious to me!" she answered.

"No? Perhaps one has to be a man to see them."

Ruth suppressed a smile. Whatever he might say, she was grateful to him for not looking miserable at the prospect of a lifelong liaison with her. That, she thought, was true gallantry!

"I—I shan't hold you to anything," she managed to say.

His expression became distant and she was more than ever conscious of his broken nose. "Won't you? Well, you can be sure that I shall hold you to your promises. There is no going back, Ruth. The outcome was inevitable from the moment you set foot on Sicilian soil."

Ruth straightened her back. If he was proud, so could she be. "That's my funeral! All I'm trying to say is that it needn't be yours too!"

He stiffened. "Indeed? I hope you don't mean what I think you do. In Sicily, it is the man who rules the marriage, not the whim of his wife."

She was immediately as angry as he. "You won't rule me!" she shot at him.

"Another challenge?" he asked her.

"A fact!" she muttered.

To her dismay, he chuckled. "Facts can be changed to suit oneself if one is sufficiently determined," he said.

"I am determined!" she insisted, more to boost her own morale than to convince him.

Mario smiled. His eyes searched Ruth's face, making her very conscious of her new hair-do and make-up. Did he think she looked beautiful? Or was he still longing for the obvious prettiness of Pearl? Ruth wished she knew.

"So am I determined," he said briefly. "And as no house can stand if it is divided against itself, I am afraid that one of us will have to give way, and it will not be me."

"Because you are a man and I a woman?"

"Exactly!" He sounded amused. "It is sometimes easier for a woman to be generous," he added.

Ruth's eyes mocked him. "Whoever told you that?" she demanded.

"Why, you did!" he answered simply, completely taking the wind out of her sails.

"*I* did!" she repeated in complete disbelief.

"Not in words," he admitted. "But if you truly believe in equality, then I can only think it is generosity that makes you offer to be faithful yourself while offering me my freedom. I should never make *you* such an offer!"

Ruth's cheeks reddened. "It wasn't an *easy* offer to make," she began, her words tripping over themselves in her embarrassment.

"But for me," he drawled softly, "the offer would have been so difficult to make, I should not have made it at all."

It was a lesson to her, she thought, not to cross swords with him. "Then I withdraw the offer," she said with dignity.

The crack of his laughter made her jump. "An honourable withdrawal?" he inquired softly.

Her own lips twitched. "It's better than an ignominious defeat," she told him.

He feigned a shudder. "Infinitely better!" he agreed. "It gives us a chance of calling a truce for the afternoon. Well, *Signora Verdecchio?*"

She offered him her hand in silent agreement. It was better, she thought, to rest her fire until she really needed it. Besides, she needed time to accustom herself to her new circumstances, so that her heart didn't jump like a clap of thunder every time anyone called her by her married name.

Ruth saw her husband through new eyes that afternoon. He sent the chauffeur away and drove his own car, pointing out the improvements he had made locally as they went.

"The roads were mostly improved by the Fascists," he told her. "It was one of the good things they left behind them. Before, when you went through the fruit-growing

76

districts, all the orchards were walled in, but the Fascists forced the people to dismantle them and now you can drive for miles through lovely scenery."

"But you're not old enough to remember Mussolini," she said.

"Just about!" he grinned.

She wanted to ask him how old he was, but she didn't dare. She turned her attention to the countryside they were driving through.

"Mario, I must send a telegram to Pearl," she said at last. "She'll be worrying about me." She twisted her fingers together nervously. "I won't let you talk me out of it," she continued quickly. "I left her some money and a note saying I would be back in a day or so. It—it isn't fair not to contact her!"

"But of course!" he responded politely. "We shall stop at the next post office we come to. You can send your message from there."

"I'm sorry to be a nuisance," she gulped. "But you do see, don't you?"

"I have said so," Mario answered. "As a matter of fact I telephoned to her yesterday, so she will not be as worried as you think."

"*You* telephoned her?"

"Why not?"

It was impossible to tell him why not when she thought about it. She only knew that she bitterly resented his having done any such thing.

"It was for me to tell her," she said. "She is my sister!"

He smiled faintly. "I don't think she'll feel particularly sisterly when next she sees you," he remarked.

"What do you mean?" she asked, puzzled.

His smile widened. "She is used to being the pretty sister!" he reminded her.

Ruth took a deep breath. "That isn't kind!" she said.

"Why not? Can't I pay compliments to my wife if I like?"

She shook her head. "I don't think it was a compliment," she said.

He was taken aback by the accusation. "It was intended as one," he assured her earnestly.

"To Pearl?" she retorted.

"No," he admitted with disarming candour, "perhaps not. I find it difficult to remember that you and Pearl are sisters—"

"I know," Ruth interrupted him. "We are so unalike."

"Well, so you are!" he told her, annoyed. "Tell me about your own mother, Ruth. Was she like you?"

Ruth shook her head. "I hardly remember her," she answered vaguely. "I remember my father marrying again, but that's about my earliest memory."

"And then along came Pearl," he said dryly.

"Why not? She was welcome!"

He smiled and said no more, but his questions had set a whole train of thought in motion. She snuggled into the comfort of the car seat and allowed her mind to wander back to her earliest childhood. She hadn't welcomed Pearl, she remembered. She had bitterly resented her arrival, for Pearl had been the most perfect baby that anyone in the Arnold circle had ever remembered. Her golden locks and bright blue eyes had been an advantage even then. Ruth, who had been only average even at that age when it came to looks, had watched her little sister twist their father round her little finger and she had been hurt when she herself had been ignored.

But Ruth had been clever. When Pearl had been collecting her first string of boy-friends, Ruth had been collecting diplomas. She had even wondered what Pearl had seen in the juvenile young men who had practically overrun the house. She herself had ruthlessly suppressed any like interest that she might have felt. She had her work and that was enough for her.

In the last two days it had not been enough, she admitted to herself. She cast a sidelong look at Mario, marvelling that his hawk-like features should have made her so vulnerable. His nose was undoubtedly too big, she decided, and his mouth, when he was not amused, could be cruel. But quite why he should stir up such a hornets' nest inside her, she couldn't imagine. He wasn't her type any more than she was his.

They came to Potella di Mare, once famed for the violence of its footpads, but now no more than a row of yellow, pink and blue houses against a backdrop of orchards. The inevitable group of children came running out to look at the car, admiring its smooth lines with all the volubility of their elders. Mario flung the eldest amongst them a coin to look after it from the thieving fingers of his friends and strode off down the straggling street, in search of a post office.

When he came back, Ruth had finished composing her message to Pearl on the back of an envelope. It was the most difficult thing she had ever written. How did you tell your sister that you had married the man she thought she was in love with? Ruth had compromised in the end by not admitting the marriage at all.

NOT RETURNING NAPLES. INSTEAD SENDING MONEY FOR YOUR RETURN PASSAGE ENGLAND. LETTER FOLLOWING. LOVE RUTH.

She had written the message carefully, printing the letters so that it could be easily read by the post office official. It was unlikely, she thought, that he had ever had to send a wire in English before in such a small place.

"Is it far?" she asked Mario as he lounged elegantly against the car, his forearms resting on the open window beside her.

"No," he said. "I sent the telegram while I was there."

She looked up at him in quick anxiety. "What did you say?"

"That I'd be in Naples tonight and would look her up," he said quietly.

"But you can't!" Ruth exclaimed.

"Why not?" he returned. "There are other boats besides the one to Tunis."

Ruth bit her lip. "That isn't what I meant," she admitted. "Won't—won't people think it odd if you go tonight?"

His eyes met hers. "It isn't their business," he said dismissively. "I will go to Naples tonight and bring Pearl back with me tomorrow."

"I'll go with you," she said doggedly.

But he shook his head. "One of us has to stay to entertain our guest," he told her.

"What guest?" she demanded.

"My aunt."

"But she's hardly a guest!" Ruth protested. "I'm not joking, Mario. If you go to Naples, I'm going with you!"

"Another challenge?" he asked her.

"Yes, if you like," she said bravely.

His smile disarmed her. "I had thought you could be happy in my house. Is that not true, Ruth?"

She didn't want to answer the question. It struck too near home. If she admitted that there was nothing she wanted more than to live in his house and be his wife, it would be all the more humiliating to know that he hadn't chosen her out of love, but because his Sicilian notions of honour had forced him to. That was bad enough! But that he should bring Pearl to his home too—Pearl, who flitted in and out of love as easily as she breathed, but who would resent having any man taken from her!

"You can't do it!" she exclaimed bitterly.

"What can't I do?"

"I will not have Pearl brought here!" she said clearly.

"I think you have no choice," he retorted silkily.

"But I do! I didn't want to be, but I am your wife! Surely I have some say in who is and who is not invited to the house!"

He didn't answer immediately. He walked round the car and got in beside her. His face was bleak and unyielding.

"I think I shall take you home," he said finally.

"I don't want to go home!" She knew that it was a childish response and promptly wished it unsaid. But she didn't want to go home. The truce between them had been so short, and now it was worse than it had been before. However, it was nothing to cry about, she told herself sharply. Tears would be the final humiliation.

Mario gave her a distant look. "I think perhaps you are more like your sister than I had supposed."

"Oh?" she said, her voice every bit as cold as his.

"I believe that you came to rescue your sister from me—"

"I did!" She blinked. "I see now that it wasn't a very sensible thing to do—"

"Sensible!" he cut her off. "That's the point. Your sister was well aware that I had no intention of marrying *her*. Is that why you came?"

Ruth stared down at her fingers, saying nothing.

"Is it?" he demanded. He grasped her by the arm and shook her, but she still said nothing. "You may as well tell me! I'll get the truth out of Pearl easily enough if you don't!"

"You're welcome to try," Ruth said fiercely.

"I will!" he blazed at her.

"Then perhaps you'll let me go," she said with dignity. "You're bruising my arm!"

He released her, but only to start up the car. She expected him to drive straight back to Palermo, but he didn't. He drove fast in the opposite direction, down the hill, across the level crossing and into Misilmeri, the small country town that had once been *Menzil-el-Emir*, 'the quarters of the Prince', when the Moors had founded the place centuries before. Now, it had forgotten its Arab antecedents. Down the centre of the town ran the main street and to either side countless alleys ran up the steep slopes of Gibilrossa. Ruth thought they might stop there, but Mario hardly seemed aware that the town existed. He barely altered their pace at all as they continued down the hill to the bridge below. On either side of the road were fields spread with vines and olives, wilting under the hot sun, but rich and verdant in comparison to the dried out land of much of southern Italy.

The gradient upwards was now so steep that even Mario's car protested at the treatment it was receiving. Ruth thought the engine might boil, but Mario remained unconcerned and forced his way up to the top. There the car came to a shuddering stop.

"Have you ever seen a better view than this?" Mario demanded.

Ruth looked back the way they had come, across the fields of vines and sun-ripened corn, the dusty leaves of the olive trees etched in green on the scorched land that formed their background. It was certainly the best view of Misilmeri, or of any town that she had ever seen. The ruins of the medieval castle that topped the town stood cut against the magnificent mountainous scenery. Beyond, she could catch a glimpse, here and there, of the blue waters of Palermo. In another direction lay the Capo Zafferano and, to the east, the whole bay of Termini.

There was too much of it. Ruth secretly preferred the 'magic casement' she had discovered for herself by the cypress trees in Mario's garden.

"I suppose not," she said in answer to his question.

"Is this what you wanted?" he pressed her.

Her eyes opened wide. "No. I didn't know what Sicily would be like."

He appeared to accept that, merely shrugging his shoulders. "My temper is easily aroused," he confessed ruefully. "You had better look out!"

She smiled with sheer relief. "I don't mind," she said quite untruthfully, for she had minded very much. "I—I expect it takes getting used to," she went on sagely. "I hadn't thought that you might find it difficult too."

He cast her an amused look, and she wondered how she ever could have resented it before. Now she was so glad that he was no longer angry with her she would willingly have withstood anything else from him.

"Are you making excuses for me?"

"Oh no!" she said hastily, a little shocked. "But it is a little awkward at first, isn't it? I mean, until we get used to it."

"But you do think that you may grow used to it?" he asked innocently.

"I don't know," she confessed, wishing that she could lie as easily as Pearl did whenever it suited her. "I—I'll try to."

He turned to face her. "It isn't often that I apologise to anyone," he said fiercely, "but I do apologise to you, Ruth. It's a nuisance that I have to go away tonight, but I have to do something about Pearl—"

She stiffened. "I don't see why," she said.

"I feel *some* responsibility for her. Goodness knows what she's been up to in Naples by herself!"

Ruth straightened out the envelope on which she had written the telegram she had wanted to send to Pearl.

"Don't you think," she began humbly, "that it would be better if she went back to England?"

He read her telegram, his lips twisted with displeasure. "You don't know much about your sister if you think she'll meekly pack her bags and go back to England!" he told her frankly.

"But she hasn't enough money to go on staying at the hotel!" Ruth told him earnestly.

"I don't suppose she has," he agreed dryly. "The sooner I get to Naples the better!"

Ruth clenched her fists. It was Pearl, Pearl, always Pearl! And if she came to Sicily, she would see nothing wrong in picking up with Mario exactly where they had left off. And that Ruth didn't think she could bear.

"I won't allow it!" she cried out. "You have no right—"

He eyed her with a haughty dislike that chilled her to the marrow.

"As your husband," he reminded her brutally, "I have any rights that I choose to take!"

CHAPTER SIX

IT was every bit as bad as Ruth had feared it might be. From the instant that Mario had informed his aunt and Giulia that he was going to Naples, their sympathy had been poured out over her.

"I had never thought it of a nephew of mine!" Lucia snapped, her eye kindling. "I shall speak to his mother about it!"

Ruth was amused despite herself at the thought of Mario paying the faintest attention to any female in his life. "I—I'm worried about my sister," she tried to explain.

Lucia's eyes grew large with disbelief. "*That* one?"

"She is a trifle feckless," Ruth admitted carefully, "but I did promise my parents that I would look after her—"

"And so you did!" Lucia reminded her with deliberate spite. "Would you be here now if it were not for her? No, of course not! If I had known that Mario would behave like this, that he would be so *unfeeling*, I should have helped you on to the first boat back to Naples myself!"

She prowled angrily up and down the *salotta*, working herself into a fine fury.

"If I don't mind," Ruth said gently, "I don't see why you should!"

The Signora looked at her shrewdly. "And I suppose you don't mind so much as a flick of your fingers!" she sneered. "It is an insult! And so I shall tell him!"

Ruth sighed. It was ironic, she supposed, that she should feel obliged to defend Mario's decision, but for some reason she did.

"Please don't!" she said with a hint of authority.

"Mario is going to Naples for me, not for Pearl, because I asked him to."

The Signora gave her a look that managed to be both pained and pitying. "You are mad, of course!" she exclaimed, lifting her hands in a helpless gesture. "There can be no other explanation! Do you think a hair-do by Luigi and a pair of fine eyes will be enough to protect you from *that one*?"

Ruth's eyes flashed. "Pearl is my sister," she reminded the older woman.

"Huh!" the Signora retorted.

"Nor is it kind," Ruth went on, warming to her theme, "to keep reminding me that I am so plain and uninteresting that no man would take a second look at me if there was any other—any other female around!"

"Female is the right word!" Lucia agreed harshly. She stopped walking up and down and laughed suddenly. *"Chi si marita in fretta, stenta adagio!* You are a fool!" she added.

Ruth's Italian might not have been very good, but she recognised the proverb easily enough. Marry in haste, repent at leisure! Well, so she probably would, but she wasn't going to lay bare her wounds for everyone's inspection if she could help it!

"I may be a fool," she said with dignity, "but I am not such a fool that I don't know that Pearl tires of anything in time."

"And you are prepared to wait?" Lucia shot at her.

Ruth lifted her chin. "I have to wait," she answered.

The Signora was considerably shaken by this exchange. She fidgeted with the ornaments on the bookcase, her rather fine face flooded with the concern she was feeling.

"I was quite wrong to help to put you in this position!" she burst out at last. "I thought it was a fine thing for the family, not that my nephew would see fit to insult you on your wedding night!"

Ruth gave a chuckle. "Would it be better on any other night?" she asked innocently.

The Signora gaped at her. "You can *laugh* about it?" she demanded.

"Why not?" Ruth returned placidly.

Lucia could easily have struck her. Much excited, she wrung her hands together with increasing energy. "It is no laughing matter! *I* shall speak to Mario myself before he goes!"

"No," Ruth said quickly. "No, please don't do that!"

Lucia looked at her suspiciously. "Why not? I suppose you helped him pack his bag?"

Ruth blushed. She preferred not to think about the exchange she had with Mario while he had been finding a pair of pyjamas to put in the briefcase that was all he was taking with him. It had been she, she remembered, who had flung open the door between their two rooms, and it had been he who had closed it again with a gentle finality that had reduced her to tears.

"Not exactly," she said.

"Then you do mind?" Lucia insisted.

Ruth rose to her feet. "I never said I didn't," she reminded the Italian woman quietly.

"Where are you going?" Lucia demanded, highly put out at the prospect of losing her audience.

Ruth smiled slowly. "To say goodbye to Mario!"

Lucia glared at her. Her eyes began to twinkle in response to the decidedly humorous look in Ruth's. "What ever happened to your fine ideas of equality?" she sighed.

Ruth shrugged. "We'll see," she said. "I may have lost the battle, but the war is only just beginning!"

Lucia looked at her with a dawning respect. "I believe you mean it!" she gasped.

"Certainly I mean it," Ruth assured her. "I may be plain, but nobody has ever accused me of being poor-spirited!"

She whisked out of the door before Lucia could think of any suitable retort, well pleased with herself for showing Signora Verdecchio that she was not the poor little dab of a thing that she thought her. But if her conversation with Mario's aunt did wonders for her self-respect, her memory of what had passed between herself and Mario made her thoroughly miserable again.

There was nothing for it, though, she decided, but to put as good a face as possible on it and hope for the best when she said goodbye to him. She couldn't prevent the hot colour flooding into her cheeks when she heard him coming down the stairs, but she forced herself to stand quite still as she waited for him.

"I hope you will tell Pearl that the invitation to stay here comes from us both?" she said as calmly as she could.

Mario glanced at her, noting the courageous lift to her head and the fright in her eyes as if she were afraid he would slap her.

"Does it come from us both?" he countered.

She winced. "Yes," she said violently.

His arms went round her and he held her close. "She has to come here, *piccina*," he whispered. "I wouldn't leave you otherwise!"

Ruth hoped that she wasn't going to cry again. She thought she might if he kissed her, but he didn't. He patted her cheek, his mind already on other things. "I'll tell Pearl she's welcome!" he said.

It wasn't quite how she would have put it, Ruth thought wryly, but it was better than his leaving on the terrible note they had struck upstairs. Ruth wished she hadn't argued with him at all! It had been bad enough in the car, when he had told her exactly what her future role as his wife would be. It had added up to a pretty dismal picture of a sterile relationship that would lead precisely nowhere. She was hardly at fault, she thought, if she had decided that it was not enough for her!

Only she hadn't contented herself with telling him that if he had rights, it meant he had duties too! She had had to involve Pearl too, making him angry all over again.

"I have the right *and* the duty to protect my sister-in-law and to invite her to stay in my house!" he had shouted at her.

"But you can't do that to me!" she had sobbed.

"Why not? She's *your* sister! You shouldn't have left her stranded in Naples," he had told her.

"Nor should you have seduced her!"

He had laughed unkindly at that. "I didn't seduce her—"

"No, but you would have done!" she had observed unwisely.

"I fancy that is my business!" he had retorted. "And perhaps hers," he had added with a touch of amusement.

"But not mine?" she had asked him painfully.

"No," he had said baldly, "not yours!"

"And I suppose it won't be my business when you bring her here?" she had gone on, knowing by his face that she was treading on dangerous ground.

"I imagine that you don't want me to answer that?" he had inquired coldly.

She had known that it was a mistake to say anything more, but she was too angry to care.

"You don't have to!" she had challenged him.

He had stood in the open doorway and had looked at her. "Don't try me too far," he had advised her. "I haven't previously believed in wife-beating, but you are fast converting me!"

"You wouldn't dare!" she had gasped.

"Try me and see!" he had retorted coolly. And he had shut the door, effectively ending the argument.

Ruth hadn't dared to open the door again. Instead, she had sat on the edge of her bed and had allowed the tears to stream unchecked down her cheeks. It had been all of half an hour before she had moved again and then she had come to a painful decision. She was Mario's wife, not from his choice or from hers, and it was up to her to make the fact as pleasant for both of them as she could. And if that meant accepting Pearl in her husband's house, then she would, and it was with this intention in mind that she had gone into the hall to bid Mario goodbye.

When Mario had gone, Ruth went back into the *salotto* to find Lucia. She felt weak and more than a little exhausted after the events of the day, but it was far too early yet to retire to her bed.

"Has Mario gone?" Lucia asked her, obviously trying to introduce a note of normality into the evening.

Ruth followed her lead with gratitude. "I think so." She smiled at her aunt-by-marriage. "When will you have to go back to Tunis?

Lucia jumped. "I ought to be there now!" she wailed. "My husband will be going up in smoke! But today, how could I go? And tomorrow evening the village will hold a *festa* for you and Mario." She looked down at her black dress with distaste. "I know I am in mourning and can't dance, but I can't bear to miss it! Roberto will understand."

It was the first Ruth had heard about it, but, when she thought about it, she supposed that she might have known that the whole place would celebrate Mario's wedding when they got to know about it.

"I suppose Mario knew all along!" she said sharply.

Lucia looked surprised. "But of course! Didn't he mention it to you? He must have done!" She giggled to herself. "He knew better than to be away tomorrow night!" she said.

So that was why he had gone to Naples on their wedding night, Ruth thought. But why, oh, why hadn't he told her?

Saro was already camped out on her bed when she went upstairs. He flapped his tail idly from one side to the other by way of greeting, sure of his own welcome.

"It's a good thing Mario isn't here to see you!" Ruth told him severely, but the small dog was unimpressed. He licked her fingers, scratched, and curled up for the night in a businesslike manner.

"Just as well!" Ruth reiterated.

But what she couldn't understand was why the dog's presence did nothing to dispel the immense feeling of loneliness that had engulfed her.

Giulia's morose expression as she served the lunch was enough to try anyone's patience. Lucia watched her with an increasing annoyance which she vainly tried to hide.

"Aren't you looking forward to the *festa*?" she asked her at last.

"No," Giulia grunted.

"But it will be a great occasion—"

Giulia sniffed. "The Signor is not even here," she pointed out. "And what will the new Signora wear? Tell me that! She has nothing in that small suitcase of hers for such an evening! It will be a disgrace to our house!"

Lucia was appalled. She turned impulsively to Ruth. "Oh, my dear, I hadn't thought! What will you wear?"

"I don't know," Ruth returned lightly. "I haven't got a wedding dress, or anything like it! What sort of thing should I wear?"

Lucia looked grave. "Something a little grand. Giulia, what would you say the Signora should wear?" Ruth was so surprised at being referred to by such a title that she scarcely paid any attention to Giulia's reply.

"I have an evening dress, if that will do?" she said suddenly.

"Perhaps we should see it," Lucia said doubtfully. "Tell Giulia where it is and she can fetch it."

"M-Mario is bringing it with him," Ruth stuttered. "He's picking up the rest of my luggage as well as Pearl."

"Then it will be crushed," Lucia said, immediately practical. "But that is a small thing. Tell me about this dress? It is modest, yes? Such as a married woman might wear?"

Ruth wasn't sure how to answer that. "I suppose so," she compromised. "I wore it once for the school dance—"

Lucia's horror made her want to laugh. "It is obviously impossible!" the Italian lady snapped. "We must go into Palermo at once and fetch another!"

But Ruth shook her head. "It's not too bad," she assured her. "And it *is* mine. I don't want Mario to have to pay for anything for me and I haven't got enough money to buy one for myself."

Lucia took a deep breath. "I shall buy it!" she announced. "I must give you something for your wedding, why not that?"

"Because," Ruth explained patiently, "you paid Luigi yesterday, and that must have cost a small fortune!"

"Luigi is not cheap," Lucia agreed justly. "Nevertheless, it is the honour of the family which is at stake. Roberto, my husband, will give you the dress!"

But Ruth was adamant in her refusal. She would wear her own dress or nothing.

"It's quite nice really," she comforted Lucia. "My parents like it," she added persuasively. "And with my new hair-style it will be an absolute knock-out!"

Lucia was obliged to admit that the new hair-style had given Ruth both style and elegance, but she was worried about the dress and there was no denying the fact. All eyes would be on Ruth that evening. For years, his people had waited for Mario to marry. He was important to them in many ways. His house was the biggest in the village. He owned most of the surrounding land, which meant that most of them worked for him in one capacity or another. And it was he who had brought other work into the area, making a real contribution to their living standards and keeping the worst excesses of the Mafia away from the district. His wife was bound to be important to them too. On her would depend the advances in women's education, the new clinics for the children, so many, many things that would thrive and prosper if her example was the right one, or wither and die if they saw that she ignored them. Did Ruth understand these things?

"We will speak to Mario about it," Lucia compromised.

Ruth's cheeks coloured. "I'll decide for myself how I dress and what I do!" she said grandly.

Lucia sighed. "But there are so many things you do not know——" she began.

"Then I shall find them out for myself!" Ruth retorted.

She might have expanded her theme of how she could look after and manage by herself, but Giulia came hurrying into the room and began clearing away the plates.

"The Signor's car has been seen!" she exclaimed excitedly. "He will be here in a few moments!" She gave Ruth an odd look. "They say he has a young woman with him. That would be your sister?"

Ruth met her disapproval face to face. "I expect so," she said gently. "Pearl is very fair and rather beautiful."

Giulia made a disparaging face. "They say she is so fair she is almost transparent!" she muttered. "That she has never seen the sun like normal folk!"

'They' seemed to have seen a great deal, Ruth reflected ruefully. She gave Lucia a humorous look. "Poor Pearl! Can it be that Sicilians don't like the very fair look?"

"It is too unusual to be considered pretty by the peasants," Lucia was forced to agree, "but there are other men!"

Ruth knew that she was referring to Mario, but for once the fact didn't disturb her. She would love the Sicilians for ever, she thought, just because they didn't like Pearl's fair looks! And if that showed how ill-natured she had become, she thought she could quite easily learn to live with it!

"Shall we go out into the drive to meet them?" Lucia suggested.

Ruth agreed with alacrity. She was, she realised, a complete fool, but she was longing to cast her eyes over Mario again, no matter if he was still angry with her, no matter what! She could hardly wait to see his tall figure, his haughty, arrogant expression, and that touch of the devilish that his broken nose supplied.

From the front door, Ruth could see the trail of dust that marked the car's progress towards them. She envied Lucia who made no secret of the fact that she was impatient with waiting and was in a fidget for them to arrive. She herself forced herself to stand completely still and hoped that the fact that she was trembling would not be visible to anyone else.

Pearl jumped out of the car as soon as the wheels

stopped moving. She looked about her with keen satisfaction, completely ignoring her sister.

"Is all this really yours, Mario?" she breathed, very impressed.

"It belongs to my family," Mario replied. Ruth wondered if she had imagined the note of impatience in his voice and decided she had when, taking Pearl by the hand, he led her up to his impatient aunt.

"This is Ruth's sister," he introduced her, adding with a grin! "She's not much like her, is she?"

Lucia extended her hand with the autocratic courtesy that any Verdecchio seemed able to assume at will. "My niece, Ruth, has spoken of you," she said distantly.

Pearl found this excessively funny. "I'm surprised she's had time," she observed artlessly. "She's been so busy, hasn't she? Running away with Mario and getting him to marry her!" Her laughing eyes passed over Mario. "And who would have thought that *he* would have been so malleable?"

Ruth felt distinctly uncomfortable. "I hope you weren't worried," she began apologetically.

Pearl looked at her at last. "You know me better than that," she said. "I never worry!"

"No, you don't," Ruth agreed doubtfully.

"Well then," Pearl advised her frankly, "there's no need to look so downtrodden. It's you who lectures me about my behaviour, not me you!"

Mario smiled down at Pearl. "Ruth has almost forgotten that she is a schoolmistress," he drawled. "You mustn't tease her!"

"Oh, I won't!" Pearl promised immediately.

Ruth hoped that Lucia's look of complete disgust was not reflected in her own face. "Shall we go inside?" she said hastily. "I'll show Pearl to her room."

"Good idea," Mario agreed. He looked tired, she

noticed with concern, and wished that she could do something about it.

"Are you coming, Pearl?" she asked her sister.

Pearl tore herself reluctantly away from Mario, blowing him a light kiss as she went.

"I see you've had your hair done," she said to Ruth as they mounted the stairs. "Was that how you did it?"

"Did what?" Ruth countered.

"Oh, let's not play games! I didn't think Mario would fall so easily, or I might have held out for marriage myself. Congratulations, sister dear!"

Ruth gave her a shocked look. "I was trying to protect you," she explained. "Pearl, I don't know how you came to give him such an impression, but the last thing Mario had in mind was marriage!"

Pearl chewed her lip thoughtfully. "If you could make it occur to him, I expect I could have done so too!"

Ruth sighed. Giulia had prepared a room for Pearl as far away from the one she was occupying as possible. Ruth had been going to argue the point with her that morning, but now she was glad she had not. It was bad enough having her in the house at all.

"I'm not very welcome, am I?" Pearl muttered, as Ruth opened the door to her room.

Ruth flushed, unwilling to admit the truth that Pearl had suddenly become very unwelcome indeed. "You're my sister, aren't you?" she replied.

Pearl giggled, "What has that got to do with it?" She walked across the room and looked out of the window, before flinging her handbag on to the bed and stepping out of her high-heeled shoes with a grimace. "Mario actually told me that you wanted me to come. And, knowing you, I almost believed him!"

"The invitation came from both of us," Ruth said flatly.

Pearl's bright blue eyes looked the picture of innocence. "You're a fool, Ruth."

Ruth smiled faintly. "Am I?"

"Did you really think that having his ring on your finger was going to stop me from taking him away from you?"

"No."

Pearl looked at her sister with a new interest. "You wouldn't have said that a couple of days ago in Naples!" she observed.

Ruth was amused. "Probably not," she agreed readily. "But I've learned a lot about us both since then."

"Us both?" It was easy to see that Pearl resented their being bracketed together in any way. "What do you mean?"

Slightly astonished that she had managed to seize the initiative so easily, Ruth said vaguely, "Oh, I don't know! I actually believed Mother that it was up to me to look after you—"

"You are the elder!" Pearl said in an aggrieved voice.

Ruth suppressed a chuckle. "In some ways," she said.

Pearl gave her a thoughtful look and then shrugged her shoulders. "If you tell Mother, I'll kill you!" she said lightly.

"It would kill her!" Ruth said warmly. "I never would have believed it! Pearl, you wouldn't really have stayed here with Mario, would you?"

Pearl looked her straight in the eyes. "It didn't seem to bother you!" she said.

"But I thought—But I didn't *know*! I was coming straight back to Naples as soon as I'd told him what I thought of him!" Ruth stammered.

"I can imagine," Pearl said with cynical amusement. "Off you went, with your little wooden sword, determined to be a martyr. Well, it's your own fault if he took you at your word—"

"But he was away!" Ruth burst out.

"*Away*! Away where?" Pearl sounded truly indignant. "Do you mean to say he didn't meet the ship?"

"No, he didn't. It would have been rather awkward if he had, for I shared a cabin with his aunt, who was expecting him to meet her. He left a message for her, telling her that a friend of theirs was seriously ill, and Lucia went there. The friend died in the night and Mario came home then, only it was too late to disturb me— you—so he waited until morning."

"Then why did he marry you?" Pearl demanded.

Ruth blushed. "He said he'd compromised me," she confessed.

"*Compromised* you!" Pearl exclaimed. "But he hadn't touched you!" She narrowed her eyes thoughtfully. "Or had he?"

"N-no." Ruth wished that she sounded more emphatic. "But this is Sicily," she went on miserably, "and he didn't think he had any choice."

Pearl uttered a scream of laughter. "Didn't you warn *me* about these customs in southern Italy?" she shrieked. "It serves you right! Or it would, if it wasn't Mario!"

"It was a trifle awkward—" Ruth admitted.

"Have you told the parents?" Pearl interrupted her. Ruth shook her head. "Then you'd better not!" Pearl went on. "It can't possibly last, and so the less they know the better."

Ruth stood her ground bravely, even as she wilted inwardly. "I don't think it can be undone very easily," she said.

Pearl stood up, losing interest in the whole conversation. "But he doesn't want you," she said scornfully. "And I shan't hold it against you! Mario and I will get along just fine without you!"

Ruth took a deep breath. "But I'm not going!" she said stubbornly.

Pearl's innocent look vanished in a flash. Ruth wondered why she had never noticed before how vindictive her young sister could look, and was immediately sorry that it should have been her who had brought such an expression to her face.

"He'll divorce you!" Pearl spat at her.

Ruth stood up very straight. "There is no divorce in Italy," she answered calmly.

Pearl looked at her sister and made a discovery. "You're in love with him!" she accused her.

Ruth blanched. "What if I am?"

"I'll still take him from you!" Pearl threatened her.

Ruth lifted her chin in a characteristic gesture. "You can try," she said. She turned on her heel and left the room, shutting the door carefully behind her. It was time to get out her dress and get ready to go to the party.

CHAPTER SEVEN

THE dress was better than she had remembered. Ruth took it out of the suitcase with loving care and laid it out on the bed. It was made of a man-made fibre that closely resembled wild silk and looked, at first glance, expensive. Closer inspection showed that it had been worn several times before and even that at one time she had had to darn a tiny hole on the hemline where her shoe had once caught in the long skirt, but that scarcely showed at all. Indeed, she liked the dusty pink colour as much now as she had ever done, and the style suited her as well as any dress she had ever had. It was not, perhaps, outrageously modish, but there was nothing frumpish about its classical lines and it was comfortable to wear.

Ruth had barely started to dress when Mario knocked on the door between their rooms. Ruth put down the hairbrush she was holding and picked up the rather skimpy bathrobe that was all she had with her. Even so, she was too late, for he had already come in. If he was embarrassed to find her in her petticoat, he didn't show it.

"Do you mind?" he asked, his eyebrows slightly raised.

"It would be all the same if I did!" she retorted.

He chuckled. "I suppose it would," he agreed. He picked up a box of powder, lavishly covered with Luigi's name, and smiled at her. "I see you took my advice," he remarked.

"Oh?" she muttered.

"Making up to your eyes!" he reminded her.

"Oh, that!" She tried to sound indifferent. "I'm glad you approve!"

He looked at her closely. "Are you?" He sat down on a stool and smiled at her. "Has Pearl settled in?"

"Yes."

"I'm sorry, *piccina*, but she had to come. You don't really doubt that, do you?"

She was undone by the gentleness of his tone. "No," she said briefly. "But I wish it wasn't so soon!"

He rose to his feet. "It won't be for long. I shall arrange for her return passage to England in a few days—"

She turned and faced him. "I shall have to tell my parents first!" she said baldly.

"That too," he agreed.

"They won't—they won't be very pleased," she told him.

The haughty look returned to his face. "I will naturally explain the circumstances to them myself," he said.

Ruth tried to imagine her father's reaction to any such tale and failed dismally. "I think I'd better tell them," she said at last.

But Mario shook his head. "It is only right that they should know the truth from me," he insisted. "If I didn't think so, it would still be the wisest course. Pearl's imagination is more torrid, I find, than any truth."

Ruth blushed. "She is rather silly—"

"But she is so pretty that nobody minds," he finished for her. "That has always been the way of the world. Any man will forgive a pretty girl much!"

Ruth was forced to admit the truth of this. It was galling, though, to hear Mario talking about her sister in such affectionate tones, especially as she could easily wring her neck for all the trouble she had caused.

"I think I'd better finish dressing," she said aloud.

He touched her dress between his fingers. "Is this what you shall wear?" he asked her.

She nodded, immediately worried that he should find it inadequate. "It's the best one I have," she said defensively. "I know it isn't new, but I like it!"

"Then I'm sure I shall like it too," he agreed calmly.

"Will you?" She bit her lip nervously. "Lucia wanted me to go into Palermo and buy a new one. It's—it's important that I should look *well* tonight, isn't it?"

"Very important, he answered calmly.

"Well then, perhaps I should have—"

"Why don't you put it on and let me see?" he suggested.

But the very idea made her dither. She hadn't finished her make-up; nor had she coaxed her hair into the new fashion Luigi had wrought for her; nor was she at all sure that she would be able to do either of these things with him standing there, watching her every movement!

"I can zip you up," he persuaded her.

She sat down in front of the dressing table and did her best to make up her face as Luigi's beautician had taught her. If her hands trembled a little, it was not surprising, she thought with a touch of indignation. She leaned back and looked at herself, noting with satisfaction that she had really managed very well. Her eyes caught Mario's in the glance and she blushed to see the warm amusement in his.

"I'm afraid whatever I do everybody's eyes will be on Pearl rather than me!" she sighed.

"Perhaps," he grunted.

"Well, they will!" she went on, getting more and more heated as she thought about the sheer injustice of it all. "They're bound to!"

"I don't know," he answered, carefully considering the matter. "It's true that she catches the eye like a flame in the dark, but she is not my wife. That too is of importance to the village. Tonight, at least, you will not be ignored, *carissima*, for your sister!"

The endearment caught her by surprise. It was so difficult to tell what he meant by it. If it were translated straight into English, she supposed it would mean 'dearest', but it had to be a much looser term in Italian or he wouldn't have used it at all.

"I don't *mind*!" she told him with dignity.

He laughed. "You are one of the few women of whom that might be true!" He held up her dress. "Are you going to put it on?"

She did so, blushing as she felt his fingers on the zip that ran up the back. When he had fastened it to his own satisfaction, he turned her round to face him and studied her carefully.

"Does it look nice?" she asked him anxiously.

"You look—beautiful " he said.

She blushed in earnest at that. "It's nice of you to say so," she said happily, "even if it isn't true."

He looked amused. "But of course it is true!" he teased her. "My judgement in these matters is never at fault! And didn't I tell you that you would be beautiful if you made up your eyes?"

She was confused and more than a little embarrassed. "You are very experienced, of course!" she rallied him.

"Do you doubt it?" he drawled.

"N-no," she admitted. "Do you think Lucia will approve?"

He smiled slowly. "Shall we go downstairs and find out?" he suggested.

It would have been hard to have felt anything else but rather special, Ruth thought, with him standing beside her. He wore his immaculate dinner jacket with an air that any man would envy. She supposed that his clothes were exceedingly expensive, for she was almost sure that the shirt he was wearing was made of silk, but even if he had hired them for the night, she couldn't imagine him looking less distinguished. Of course he was arrogant, but it was comfortable too to be with someone who was so much at home with himself and so completely sure that everything was going to work out his way.

"Don't be too sorry, my dear," he said in her ear.

She managed a tremulous smile. "Oh, but I'm not!" she assured him. "I'm even beginning to *like* knowing that I'm being discussed the length and breadth of Sicily! I assure you, life was positively *dull*, when I was quiet and respectable and I didn't know I had any honour to lose!"

He laughed. "I thought I detected something complacent about you this evening!"

She bit her lip to stop herself laughing. "Why not? Not even Sicilian bandits hold any terror for me now!"

"Did they ever?" he asked with interest.

"When I had some honour to lose!"

"Perhaps you have—" he observed, watching the colour fly up into her cheeks.

"But," she stammered, "that doesn't have anything to do with it! We—we're married—"

"I wondered when it would occur to you!"

"I think you are singularly ungallant to remind me!" she complained. To her great annoyance she saw that Mario was looking remarkably pleased with himself. "And I don't find it in the least bit funny either!" she added crossly.

His eyes lit with laughter. "You disappoint me," he said. "I was beginning to think that your spirits could rise to anything!"

"Then you must think me very stupid!" she retorted, unaccountably flattered.

"No, only rather brave," he amended. He lifted her

hand to his lips and kissed her lightly on the fingers. "Well, madame wife, shall we go down and show your dress off to the others?"

Ruth was very conscious that every eye was on her as she came slowly down the stairs, her hand lightly resting on Mario's arm. She could tell from Pearl's wide-eyed astonishment and Lucia's smothered laugh of triumph that she had never looked so well in her life before.

"Ruth!" Pearl addressed her, unable to hide her chagrin. "Would you believe that she is always lecturing *me* about wearing too much make-up!"

"It is a question of how you use it, not how much you use," Lucia explained to her kindly.

Pearl turned her back on her, looking downright sulky. Ruth thought she looked small and hurt and her heart was wrung on her behalf. She hurried down the last few stairs and went straight to her sister.

"Are you coming with us into the village?" she asked her gaily. "I think Henry Brett is bringing his jeep to take those who can't get in to Mario's car."

Pearl's attention was immediately caught. "Who is Henry Brett?" she asked.

"He is an Englishman," Mario answered her. "He is putting in a new irrigation system in the village."

Pearl's eyes fastened on him earnestly. "You are so good, Mario! I suppose you are paying for it?"

Mario was frankly embarrassed. "I have more land than anyone else which will benefit from the scheme," he said abruptly.

"I want to go in your car," Pearl pleaded with him. "You promised me that I would see your village in your company! Don't you remember?"

Ruth tried not to listen to his answer. She was helped by Henry's arrival, looking strange and uncomfortable in evening dress. He came across to her immediately, blatantly pleased to see someone else of his own nationality on what promised to be a very Italian occasion.

"You should see the traffic outside!" he told her. "They've put up lights in all the streets, and even the saints from the churches have been brought out to greet you!"

"What?" Ruth said in disbelief.

"The statues! You should see them all in their party dresses!"

Ruth laughed. "I do hope they will like me," she said, betraying her nervousness with a wry grimace.

Henry looked her up and down. "They'll like you!"

"And what about me?" Neither of them had seen Pearl come dancing up behind Henry's back, but at the sound of her voice, he turned sharply and stared at her. "I'm Ruth's sister," Pearl went on. "I don't suppose anyone has mentioned me, because I am *quite* unimportant—"

"You're the Pearl Beyond Price!" Henry muttered in a strangled voice.

"How nice of you to say so!" Pearl said coolly.

Henry grinned. "But how did you get here?"

She opened her blue eyes very wide. "Mario came to Naples last night to get me," she told him.

Henry blinked nervously. "I shouldn't tell anyone else that!" he advised her.

"Why not?" she riposted. "It's the truth!"

Henry cleared his throat thoughtfully. "I daresay Ruth was worried about you," he managed.

Pearl patted his arm affectionately. "How *nice* you are!" she said with warm approval. "Do you always think the best of everyone?"

One look at Lucia's furious face made Ruth take a quick step forward. She was touched that Mario's aunt should be so fiercely loyal to her and grateful too, but that volatile lady was highly unlikely to guard her tongue and Ruth knew from long experience how Pearl could colour anything in her own mind to suit herself. For a second, Ruth wished earnestly that she would never have to feel responsible for her young sister ever again, but then the moment passed and she remembered that Pearl had always been flattered and the centre of everyone's attention. It was too much to expect her to resign her position to anyone as ordinary and undemanding as Ruth was without something of a struggle.

"Do let's go!" Ruth said urgently.

To her relief, Mario began to collect the party together, packing them in to the cars to be taken into the centre of the village.

"I am sorry," he said to Pearl, "but you will have to go with Henry. Lucia is afraid for her dress in such a vehicle, and we must also take Giulia and her husband with us."

Pearl was prepared to argue the point. "But Giulia is the maid!" she exclaimed.

Mario's face became stiff and unyielding. It was a look Ruth felt that she was beginning to know well and she was glad that, this time, it was nothing she had done which had inspired it.

"Giulia is one of my people," he said, his voice totally devoid of any expression. "She has a right to my consideration."

Pearl flounced out of the front door. "I am beginning to feel quite sorry for Ruth!" she muttered darkly.

"You need not!" Mario retorted sharply. "She is my wife!"

Pearl pouted her dislike of the idea. "Not yet she isn't! Besides, you didn't want to marry her!"

"Pearl!" Ruth exclaimed, shocked.

"Well, it's true, isn't it?" Pearl returned, trying hard to look indifferent to the consternation she had caused.

Mario laughed, thus successfully puncturing the

highly charged atmosphere. "No, it is not true!" he said firmly. "And if it were, I hope you wouldn't be so vulgar as to dwell on it?"

"No, of course not!" Pearl said quickly.

The whole party hurried into the waiting cars. Mario handed Ruth into the front seat of his own car, but Ruth could not bring herself to look at him as she thanked him. She wondered if anyone else had noticed that he had practically accused Pearl of vulgarity, and hoped not. Ruth felt slightly sick. She had thought of Pearl as being young and helpless, even rather naïve, for so long that she found it painful to see her through other eyes.

"Pearl doesn't mean half that she says," she told him nervously as he got into the driving seat beside her.

He gave her a quick look. "As long as *you* realise that!" he said.

"She—she doesn't think!" Ruth rushed on.

"No," he agreed briefly.

"But she isn't *vulgar*!" she protested.

Mario laughed. "I find her inexpressibly vulgar," he said with calm certainty. "But she's none the worse for that!"

Ruth sighed. "I wish I could believe that," she said. "I mean, I wish I could believe that you didn't—didn't—"

"I don't!" Mario answered, irritated. "One does not marry vulgarity, however," he added crushingly.

Ruth was hurt on Pearl's behalf. She wished she understood better, but Mario was an enigma to her. How could he insist on going to Naples to bring Pearl to his home on the one hand, when he didn't respect her at all, or so it seemed to Ruth, on the other? Ruth couldn't imagine liking anyone that she didn't respect, and yet he seemed to find it the easiest thing in the world!

The village was indeed *en fête*. Lucia eyed the coloured lights and the bonfires with intense satisfaction from the back of the car.

"What a pity it is," she said, "that we couldn't make all the old ceremonies for you!"

"It depends—" Ruth began.

"Nonsense!" Lucia said firmly. "They were very pretty customs! You will find out tonight!"

Ruth looked at Mario, her anxiety clear in her eyes. "You will stay close, won't you?" she pleaded.

"As much as I can," he assured her. "But tonight everyone will want to dance with the bride!"

Ruth was silent. It would leave him free to dance with Pearl, she thought, and wondered why she disliked the idea so much.

"But there are other things!" Lucia put in quickly. "There is the wedding dinner, many things!"

It seemed to Ruth that there was hardly room for them to push their way into the central square. The church was lit up on the one side and the fountain was playing with gay abandon on the other, while the children splashed in and out of it, dyeing the water bright red as an emblem of marriage. Somehow, the people were pushed back to make room for the cars and the priest himself opened the door for Ruth to alight. She hesitated for a minute, waiting for Mario as he came round the car and took her firmly by the hand. The buzz of excited noise in the crowd came to an abrupt end as one old woman, and then another, stepped forward and threw a handful of corn over their heads. Because Mario stood there with his head proudly held aloft, Ruth did so too, though the dust from the chaff got into her eyes and she began to wonder whether they weren't going to be buried in the stuff.

"I'm sorry there's so much of it," Mario said in her ear. "Traditionally, only our mothers do this, but they are not here and we seem to have acquired rather a lot of substitutes!"

Ruth laughed. Truth to tell, she was beginning to enjoy herself. The heat and light from the bonfires attracted her and she loved the lined, leathery faces of the old women as they pressed in close to her. She thanked them all in her broken Italian, willingly grasping their hands as they shouted their good wishes into her ear.

The procession moved slowly but inexorably towards one end of the square where some trestle tables had been laid ready. The priest went anxiously ahead of them, clearing a path for them to travel towards the top of the centre table.

"You must sit here," he told them.

"And taste the honey!" an old man called to them.

It was Mario's turn to laugh. He dipped a spoon into the pot of honey on the table and held it out to Ruth. "Only half, mind!" he told her as her lips closed over it.

Her eyes danced. "What happens if I take more than my share?"

"I haven't the remotest idea!"

He licked the spoon clean and joined in the laughter around them. The people pressed forward, all of them anxious to get a seat at the table where Mario and Ruth were sitting.

The meal that followed was a sumptuous affair. Ruth thought that the women must have spent the greater part of the day preparing it and was touched that they should take so much trouble. It was true that it was Mario's money that had probably paid for it all, but it couldn't pay for the love and esteem they had showered on him, and therefore on his wife, that night.

Two dishes in particular seemed to be essential to the feast: a thick kind of macaroni, called *maccarruna di ziti*, and stewed pork. Ruth was reminded immediately that both the Romans and the Etruscans had eaten pork at weddings and she liked the idea that the custom should have survived through so many centuries and changes. It made her feel more a part of the island of Mario's people.

"When the wedding supper is held at home, plates of macaroni are sent to every household in the neighbourhood," Mario told her. "At least that won't be necessary tonight!"

Ruth glanced over to where Pearl was sitting. Her sister sat over the table, with her head drooping over hunched shoulders, picking at the food in front of her. She looked the picture of misery and Ruth felt uneasy at the sight. Sooner or later, if Pearl was unhappy, someone else would be called upon to pay the bill, and, just tonight, she didn't want it to be her!

Mario's glance followed Ruth's eyes. "I'll get Henry to dance with her as soon as the music begins," he promised.

Ruth nodded. It wasn't Henry that Pearl wanted to dance with, but she could hardly say so. She looked away and tried to forget all about her, but she couldn't. Wherever she looked, there was Pearl, hunched up and miserable, and accusing Ruth in her misery because she had stolen Mario from her and was sitting beside him only because she was a cheat and a fraud.

And it was all true! Ruth gulped and choked. Mario cast her an anxious look and poured her out some wine.

"Why must you worry so much?" he asked her gently. "Do you think I cannot protect my wife?"

She shook her head. "No," she admitted.

"Well then?" he prompted her.

"You might not want to," she said diffidently.

He was plainly astonished. "Then you do not know Sicilians! The Verdecchio family is very old and very proud. Isn't it enough for you to be one of us? Who would dare harm us?"

Ruth didn't feel able to tell him. "I expect it's the wine and the heat," she said apologetically.

"We will call it that," he agreed.

One of the other great landlords of the island, a man who had been to school with Mario and was a lifelong friend, rose to his feet, beating on the table for silence.

"What happens now?" Ruth asked, startled.

Mario chuckled. "It's as well your Italian isn't very good," he told her. "He's about to give the *canzuna*!"

She was still puzzled. "What is that?"

"A kind of nuptial ballad," he smiled. "This fellow is an expert, so beware!"

Ruth sat in a frozen silence until the last, lingering verses came to an end. Her Italian didn't need to be very good, she thought, for her to gather the general sense of the improvised ballad. The look in the eyes of his hearers was more than enough to tell her that all she had ever heard about Sicily and Sicilians was true. They were delighted with Mario's sudden romance. What better way was there to marry than to abduct one's bride and refuse to send her back? This was the way it had always been! Had not Odysseus abducted Penelope from her father, Icarius, King of Sparta? And what had been Penelope's reaction when her father had pursued them right into Ithaca? She had lowered her veil, signifying that she was going to follow her husband wherever he led! What a scandal it had been in those far off days when a man had lived with his wife's people! Yet Penelope had set a world-wide fashion, followed by the new Signora Verdecchio that very day! A man's strength should win him his bride, and Mario had done just that! Happily, some of the innuendoes passed Ruth by, but the compliments to herself were subtle and pleased her. When the ballad came to a resounding close, she was flushed and, had she known it, lovely. When her features were still, she might look plain, but when her eyes lit with excitement, she had a warmth and vivacity which other, more beautiful, women often lack.

A violin began to scrape a tune on the other side of the square and within seconds all the musicians of the village had gathered together and started to play the traditional dances of ancient Sicily : the *fasola*, the *puliciusa*, the *chiovu*, and the *papariana*. There was hardly anyone left alive who knew the steps as they should have been danced, but nobody cared. At a wedding, nobody thought about these things !

Mario stood up and held out his hand to Ruth. She followed his lead, a little self-conscious at having to begin the dance. The cobbles of the square were uneven and hardly made for dancing, but it didn't matter at all. Mario's arms went round her and, following the intricate bars of music, they matched their steps together and crossed the square, at first alone, but then with a hundred other couples, young and old, following behind them.

Mario's hands felt very strong on her back. He pulled her closer to him and she went gladly. She was no longer nervous or unhappy about the future. For this moment, she gave herself up to the exultant happiness of being his wife. Then the music came to an end and the moment with it.

"*Signore*, you may not monopolise the bride !" The laughing rebuke came between them and Mario reluctantly relinquished her to the next man in line. And so it went on, until Ruth felt she must have danced with every man there, as they each claimed the privilege of dancing with the bride.

She longed for Mario to come back and take her in his arms again, but he did not. Henry stood before her once, dancing stiffly to attention and barely in time to the music as they circled the square.

"I trust you will be very happy," he said formally when the dance wore to a close.

"Thank you," she answered demurely. She ought to say something more, she thought, but she could think of nothing that was appropriate. Her happiness lay in other hands than Henry's. She searched the crowded square for a sight of Mario, half-hoping that he would come to her. And then she saw him and he was dancing with Pearl. And even as she looked, he bent his head and kissed her sister gently on the cheek.

CHAPTER EIGHT

RUTH tried to pretend to herself that she had not noticed. She turned back to Henry with an eager smile.

"Shall we dance the next one together too?" she asked him.

"If—if you like," Henry agreed reluctantly. "But, to tell the truth, Mario has already warned me off!"

Ruth looked innocent. "I don't know what you're talking about!" she said.

"Well, there was that day when I took you round the place," he reminded her. "He didn't like it!"

Ruth felt decidedly cross. "It wasn't any of his business what I did!" she pointed out.

"He seemed to think it was!" Henry remembered. "And you weren't married to him then! He'd probably throw me out of Sicily if I so much as look at you now!"

"I don't believe it!" Ruth denied hotly. "If he felt like that, he wouldn't agree to half the island dancing with me now, would he?"

"That is customary!" Henry returned. "But nobody has more than one dance with the bride, or hadn't you noticed?"

"I can't say that I have!" Ruth said ruefully. "My feet hurt!" she added.

"Well, there you are then!" Henry said thankfully. "Why don't you sit down?"

"Because," Ruth said flatly, "I don't see why Mario should enjoy himself as he pleases if I can't!"

Henry grinned reluctantly. "Facts of life," he said.

"Oh, Henry!" Ruth exclaimed in despair.

"Don't see why you should care," Henry went on reasonably enough. "After all, he knew Pearl before he ever met you. It was a pretty low-down trick you played on him at that—"

Ruth turned on him angrily. "*I* didn't do anything! All I did was come to Sicily to tell him what I thought of him for playing about with Pearl's affections. And what happened? He forced me to marry him!"

"You know what?" Henry said wisely. "You're jealous of Pearl!"

"*I am not!*"

"I think you are," Henry went on imperturbably. "I'm not saying you haven't good reason to be, because she—well, she has what it takes, hasn't she? Anyone can see that."

Ruth eyed him thoughtfully. "Do you mean that you're attracted to her too?" she asked, almost eagerly.

He looked embarrassed. "She's immensely pretty," he said stiffly.

"Yes, isn't she?" Ruth agreed. "And she's having a miserable time really. Why don't you go and cheer her up?"

For a long moment he considered the matter. "I think I'd better not," he said at last. "I don't want to step on Mario's toes twice over!"

"*Damn* Mario!" Ruth exploded.

"Yes, well, it's all right for you," he said. "He won't do anything to you, but he was quite explicit as to what he would do to me! I wouldn't like to risk it. He looks quite civilised and reasonable, but I never knew a Sicilian yet who was when it comes to women. They'll stick a knife in you as soon as look at you if you so much as look at their sister!"

This gloomy thought seemed to depress him so much that Ruth hadn't got the heart to argue with him.

"It isn't *fair!*" she said.

But Henry wouldn't have this. "I don't think fairness comes into it," he said objectively. "I rather admire them, actually. I mean, I couldn't work myself up into a fury about nothing, if you know what I mean, but they do it with great verve and dash, don't you think? I think if I were a woman I'd be rather flattered."

Ruth missed her step, tripping over the cobbles. "*Flattered*? Henry, you don't know what you're talking about! Why should one be flattered by having to stay at home being grateful for the crumbs that fall one's way?"

He looked embarrassed. "It isn't as bad as that?"

"It seems every bit as bad as that to me!" she snapped.

"I can't see why," he objected. "If you want to know, *I* think you and Mario are very well matched!"

Ruth was shocked into silence. "*I* don't go round kissing other people," she muttered when the silence had become unbearable to her.

"But you'd like to," Henry said simply. "You'd do it just to attract Mario's attention, to see what he would do. I daresay that's why he kissed Pearl, come to that," he added darkly.

"I don't believe you!" Ruth said harshly.

"I'm not asking you to," Henry retorted, for once sure of his ground. "But I can tell you that no one will cross Mario round here, so you won't be able to try! What's more, I think it's a jolly good thing. Mario would probably beat you!"

"Just let him try!" Ruth exclaimed through gritted teeth.

"Well, I think he might," Henry affirmed.

"And yet he can do what he likes!" The blatant injustice of it all cut Ruth to the quick.

Henry had the audacity to laugh. "I think he's being rather successful," he remarked obscurely.

"Oh?" Ruth prompted him coldly.

"I should say so!" he went on blithely. "Pearl would be right out of her depth, as I am! You have to hand it to Mario, he probably spotted that from the first!"

Ruth blushed. "I don't know what you're talking about," she said haughtily.

"Oh yes, you do!" He gave her a brotherly shake. "You're silly too, if you think you can fight him and win—"

"I suppose you expect me to submit to *anything*?" she demanded fiercely.

"No, I don't," he answered promptly. "But I expect Mario does."

The music came to an end, to the relief of both of them. Ruth thanked him gravely and left him as quickly as possible. She was burning with sheer animal anger, such as she had never known in her life before. No doubt Henry thought he was being very clever, but she had never heard anyone talk so much nonsense! Why, she didn't care what Mario did *for herself*! Nor did she care what the local people thought of her! If he wanted to make a fool of himself by kissing Pearl at *their* wedding party, she didn't care!

There was one thing that Henry had said that made sense, though. Mario would only hurt Pearl in the long run. He would have broken her without even knowing that he had done so if Pearl had come to Sicily in the first place. Whereas she, Ruth, could give as good as she got any time, anywhere! She might even break him, she thought with satisfaction, for even while the rules were written differently for the man, he was still as much married to her as she was to him!

She was doubly startled when he took her by the arm and led her across the square towards where Lucia and Pearl were standing, glaring at one another in mutual dislike.

"I fancy we have both danced sufficiently duty dances," Mario said politely.

"Oh, do you think so?" She sounded doubtful. "You don't seem to have been very successful at cheering up Pearl," she added.

Mario's hand on her arm tightened. "Unworthy!" he told her.

"Not at all!" she answered. If he could be polite, so could she! "You really mustn't let my presence stand in your way!"

"I won't!" he said promptly.

He delivered her to Lucia's side and left her there, turning on his heel and walking away without another word.

"You don't know how maddening it is not to be able to dance!" Lucia told her immediately. "I never thought it could be so frustrating! Not that there is anyone here I could dance with, I suppose!"

"Why ever not?" Ruth asked, barely listening. She watched Mario walking away from herself to Pearl and wished she had kept a still tongue in her head.

"Roberto wouldn't like it," Lucia sighed. "But I *hate* having to wear black on a night like this!"

Ruth felt a rush of sympathy for her. "Do you always do what Roberto says?" she asked with interest.

Lucia's eyes shone with amusement. "No," she said. "But I like him to think that I do!"

Ruth lifted her chin. "Why?"

"Because then he is nice to me!" Lucia answered, surprised. "I *like* him to be nice to me!" she added warmly. She gave Ruth a quick look, shaking her head at her. "You make too much of too little, my dear!"

"Do I?" Ruth said uncertainly.

"Sicilians look after their property," Lucia told her gently. "Why else do they have blood feuds? If Mario's mother could understand this, why not you?"

"I am not Mario's property," Ruth said grimly.

Lucia giggled. "No? Oh, Ruth, you are so serious! Why don't you enjoy tonight and let tomorrow bring something new to enjoy?"

Ruth shrugged. "I can't!" she said frankly.

For an instant, Lucia looked sad too. "And I should be quite happy if Roberto was here!" She poured herself and Ruth each out a glass of wine and sipped it, her feet tapping in time to the music. "Young people cannot dance any more!" she exclaimed. "In my day, we knew all the steps—everything!" She glanced disparagingly at a couple dancing nearby. "Nor did we show our affection in public," she said in disapproving tones. "That was never done!" She stiffened suddenly, causing Ruth to look at her to see what was the matter. The Italian woman had gone completely white and then, ignoring the dignity that at other times she found so necessary to her, she emitted a squeal of sheer joy. "It's Roberto! *Roberto*, I am here!"

Roberto smiled across the dancers at his wife. He had a strong look of Mario, though he was of course an older man. Ruth wondered if that hawklike nose was a feature of all the Verdecchio family. She tried to pretend to herself that she found it unattractive, but her incurably honest mind rejected any such fancy out of hand, and she was left with the glaring truth that it was enough to set her heart hammering in the most uncomfortable way merely because it reminded her of Mario.

"*Roberto*!" Lucia shrieked, grasping at the cloth of his coat. "What are you doing here?"

Roberto rescued his coat and kissed his wife with careful propriety. "I thought if I were to ever see you again—"

"But I would have come home tomorrow!" Lucia protested.

"I wish I were as sure!" he reproved her. "Besides,"

he added on another note, "I wanted to dance at my nephew's wedding!"

"Oh, *can* we dance?" Lucia rattled on. "I am still in mourning, you know!"

"Seeing that your dress is black, I did know," he teased her. "Still, I think you might dance with me!" His eyes slid curiously over Ruth and then asked a question of his wife.

"This is Ruth, our new niece," Lucia said with pride. "Ruth, this is my husband, Roberto."

Ruth extended her hand and was a little startled to have it kissed. It wasn't only Roberto's nose that reminded her of Mario, she thought, it was also the rich amusement that flooded into his eyes, just as if he knew exactly what she was thinking.

"Ah, so this is our niece! I thought for a moment it was the other one."

"N-no," Lucia said hastily. "Pearl is Ruth's sister."

"That explains why she is dancing with Mario," Roberto approved. His attention was turned fully on to Ruth, who met his stare full on, lifting her chin a trifle to show that she didn't care.

"Well?" she challenged him.

"Very well," he said instantly. "But then Mario will have told you that, no?"

Honesty compelled her to admit that he had, but she wasn't going to admit it to Mario's uncle or anyone else.

"Won't you dance with Lucia?" she prompted him gently.

He raised his eyebrows. "And leave you alone? No, my dear, we can wait to dance together. Besides, I want to make your acquaintance. I think I shall join you in a glass of wine and then we can talk."

Ruth was nervous of any such plan, but she didn't feel she could complain, for he undoubtedly meant to be kind. She would have made some sort of protest when

Lucia suddenly departed, leaving them together, but something in his look prevented her.

"You're very like Mario," she confided with a quick smile.

"So I believe," he agreed. "But then all the Verdecchios have a look of each other." He raised his glass to her. "Shall we drink to many future Verdecchios?"

Ruth blushed. "If—if you like," she stammered.

"It is a great sadness to us both that Lucia and I have no children," he went on in the same calm tones. "It makes us more interested in Mario, perhaps, but we don't mean to interfere."

Ruth thought that she detected some kind of question in his words and rushed to Lucia's defence. "Your wife has been kindness itself to me!" she insisted. "She's a darling!"

He looked amused. "Well, I think so," he said. "Shall we dance?"

She was relieved to discover that when he was dancing, Roberto was not at all like Mario. He barely touched her he held her so lightly and anyway the music was slower now and much easier to follow so there was less need to follow his lead as closely as she had had to do earlier in the evening when the steps had been strange to her.

"Is Mario being kind to you?" he asked her suddenly.

Ruth came to a full stop in the middle of the square. "Yes, he is," she said defensively.

"Does he know you are in love with him?" he went on conversationally.

Ruth pulled herself free of him. "I don't think you have any right to ask that!"

He began to dance again, considering her thoughtfully. "You may be right," he said at last, then he smiled slowly. "You must not tell Lucia, but you, my dear, are the reason I have come to Sicily. I had a telephone call from New York, from Mario's mother. She was worried about you."

"About *me*?"

He nodded gravely. "She too was a stranger once to Sicily and she felt that somebody ought to look after you, to be on your side—"

Ruth felt the tears well into her eyes and was afraid that she was going to cry. She sniffed instead and forced herself to smile. "Was she—was she kidnapped too?" she asked faintly.

He laughed and shook his head. "She was a very willing captive," he remembered. "Are you?"

"Is that what she asked you to find out?" Ruth said pathetically, shaken by Mario's mother's concern for her.

"More or less. She said you were not to be forced against your will whatever Mario might say. And she wanted to know other things about you too," he added.

Laughter crept into Ruth's eyes. "Like whether I am respectable and—and the sort of girl Mario *ought* to marry?" she pressed him.

"Something like that," he admitted. "She had heard some quite alarming stories about some girl he was taking about in Naples—"

"From Lucia!" Ruth sighed.

Roberto grinned. "I have never known a woman who didn't gossip!" he defended his wife.

"And what will you tell Mario's mother?" Ruth asked him.

"What would you like me to tell her?"

Ruth was embarrassed. "I—I don't know," she said at last. She looked up at him and made a decision. "Yes, I do. Will you tell her that being married to Mario is like being married to a tiger? It's dangerous, but it makes anything else seem dull by comparison!"

He laughed heartily at that. "She will appreciate your choice of simile!" he assured her. "And I shall tell her, too, that you are a very nice girl," he promised. "It may even stop her taking the next aeroplane across the Atlantic to see for herself!"

"Would it matter if she did?" Ruth asked him curiously.

"I think she would worry to find your sister here with you," he said gently. "Mary-Anne would not understand that you might like having her with you. She would undoubtedly hatch some plot to have her removed!"

Ruth gasped. It was so very much what she would have liked to do herself, only she hadn't the courage actually to do anything of the kind.

"Should I like her, do you think?" she enquired, because for some reason it was very important to her that Mario's mother would like her.

"I think so," Roberto said, amused, and glanced at his watch. "I think I shall just have time for a dance with Lucia before we shall have to start going home. Come, my dear, I shall take you to Mario."

A movement ran through the crowd as the evening came to an end. The bonfires had almost burnt themselves out and the musicians were too tired to play for much longer. Only the fountain went on playing with as much gusto as ever, using the same water over and over again. But, at a signal from Roberto Verdecchio, every man there produced a hand-made torch which they lit in the dying embers of the fires. It was a beautiful sight, their sunburned, copper-coloured faces reflected in the orange light of the flames.

Mario turned to Ruth as the last dance came to an end. "I think we are going to be escorted home," he said dryly.

"A procession?" she asked.

"It used to be the custom. I thought it was dying out. I suppose we shall just have to put up with it," he added.

But Ruth was quite excited by it all. "It's beautiful!" she exclaimed.

Mario gave her a warm look. "Then we shall do our best to enjoy it!" he said with zest. "It is not every day that I lead my wife home!"

It was, Ruth thought, a curious custom. The family gathered at the head of the column with herself and Mario in the lead. Behind them came the entire village, carrying their flaring torches to light up the darkness of the road back to the Verdecchio house.

With her hand tucked into Mario's arm, Ruth walked beside him down the street that led away from the square. The night was as black as velvet, lit by a moon of such gigantic proportions that she wondered if it were going to storm on the morrow. Perhaps, though, in the humid heat of the summer, it was often like that, vivid and orange like a golden soverign. A faint wind blew up the street, stirring the skirts of her dress. With it came the distinctive smells of the village : the grey dust, garlic, the vinegary smell of wine, and the earthy scent of the plants that lined the balconies.

"Does it feel like home?" Mario asked her.

She was astonished that he should have read her mind so exactly. "In a way," she said.

He laughed. "It is a good night for bandits!" he teased her.

"You forget," she retorted with dignity, "I am not afraid of bandits!"

"Have you no qualms at all? What if a Sicilian bandit should jump out at us this minute?"

She refused to be disturbed. "With the whole village looking on?" she murmured. "Besides," she added, "I have you to protect me!"

He looked at her, but it was too dark for her to see what he was thinking. "Remember that!" he said.

They left the village behind them and walked through the vineyards. They were nearly home.

"My uncle Roberto appears to approve of you," Mario said, half-laughing. "Did my mother send him?"

Ruth forbore to answer. "I like him very much," she said instead.

"Do you?" He was silent for a minute. "You like us all, don't you?"

"Yes," she answered truthfully.

He sighed. "It is not a Sicilian emotion," he said at last. "To us an emotion is scarlet, jet black, or white. We never dwell in the pale greys!"

If she were honest, Ruth thought, she would have to tell him that she didn't either. In the past, she might have done, but only because she had never known any other.

"How exhausting for you!" she said with a smile.

"How English of you!" he retorted.

"Why not? I am English," she reminded him.

He laughed at her, and she discovered that she liked it. "A quibble! An accident of birth!" he teased her.

Her heartbeat quickened. Did he *know*? "That reminds me," she said practically, in a voice that wobbled woefully nevertheless. "I must take my passport to the British Consul—"

"I will do it for you tomorrow," he cut her off. His voice was as cold and withdrawn as ever and her spirits sank accordingly. Somehow she had managed to ruin the moment and not even their arrival at the house could make up for the lost opportunity. And she didn't know when there would be another—There might never be another! She knew a moment's panic and dreaded having to walk through the front door into the revealing light. She was tired and she felt defeated, and she didn't think she could hide either fact for long from Mario's searching eyes.

Mario's people pressed closely round them as they stood on the doorstep and faced the circle of proud faces. There was laughter as he slipped his arm round Ruth's waist, and more when he kissed her on the cheek.

"Goodnight," he called out to them.

"Goodnight! Sleep well!" they answered with meaning.

The door opened behind them and Ruth hurried into the hall, bitterly aware of the colour in her cheeks.

"I'm going to find Saro," she mumbled to Mario. "Giulia shut the back door, so he won't have been able to get in by himself."

He stood at the foot of the stairs, irritated and yet withdrawn. "I should have thought he could have slept in the stables!"

"But I like his company!" she insisted.

"You will spoil him! He is not a lap-dog. His job is to catch rats in the outhouses. How can he do that if you will bring him into the house?"

Ruth eyed him defiantly. "I don't believe he ever kills *anything*!" she muttered.

"Then we had best get another dog!" Mario said with crushing effect.

"Then Saro can be my dog!"

Mario's expression softened. "If you like," he agreed. "You have probably already ruined him for his job."

Ruth didn't wait for him to change his mind. She rushed through the kitchen, pretending to herself that she was truly anxious for the dog, when she knew quite well that she would have jumped at any chance to get away from Mario until she had sorted out the chaotic emotions that seethed within her. She was not helped by the almost liquid quality of the night air and the sound of song from the villagers, serenading them from the front garden. It was a bitterly ironic moment, for she couldn't think how happy she would have been if all their good wishes had come true.

The dog came out from his hiding place at the first sound of her voice, his tail lashing his sides in his enthusiasm and delight. He ran before her into the kitchen, ignoring Giulia's wail of anguish as she saw him, and rushed on up the stairs, pausing only to scratch softly at the door of Ruth's room.

"I take him out!" Giulia shouted up the stairs. "I come now!"

Ruth smiled down at her. "No, leave him," she pleaded. "He's not doing any harm!"

Giulia went back into the kitchen, muttering imprecations under her breath. Ruth looked after her in a haze of indecision. Was it for her to make the first move? She didn't know. She caught sight of Pearl's fair head in the hall beneath her and instinctively pulled back into the shadows so that she wouldn't be seen. The singing had stopped and the villagers were going home. She could hear them calling out to one another, laughing and joking, as they went.

Saro scratched more imperatively on her door and Ruth went to let him in. He jumped up on to her bed and scratched himself with uncalled-for energy.

"You've probably got fleas!" she told him crossly.

He paid no attention. When he had finished scratching, he lay down flat on the bed and watched her every movement as she took off her dress and made herself ready for bed. She took a quick shower in the bathroom near her room, summoning up her will-power to cope with fluttering indecision that had seized her.

She had brushed her hair three times over before she came to any decision. If she was Mario's wife, she told herself, then Mario's wife she would be!

She took a deep breath to give herself courage and

went over to the communicating door between their rooms. Her hand was shaking a little as she reached out for the door knob and turned it. But the door refused to open. It was only then that she realised that he had locked it. With a rush, she flung herself on her bed beside Saro, and burst into tears. She cried until she couldn't stop and she was still sobbing when she fell asleep just before the grey light of dawn began to creep over the horizon.

CHAPTER NINE

RUTH was the last person down to breakfast next morning. She had expected a sound scolding from Giulia, who usually resented having to make coffee, or anything else, more than once, but Giulia had only wished her a good day, her whole face wreathed in smiles.

"Where is everyone?" Ruth asked her, put out by her unaccustomed attitude.

"They have already departed," Giulia answered indifferently. "The Signor would not have anyone wake you in case you were tired." She sighed gustily. "He has already gone about his business, but he said he would be back later. He has some business to do in Palermo."

Ruth poured out her coffee. "Has my sister gone out too?" she inquired.

Giulia shrugged. "How would I know?"

Ruth gave her a look of gentle reproof and the Italian woman sulkily handed her a roll of bread. "She is waiting for the Signor," she told Ruth reluctantly. "They go together to Palermo."

Ruth winced. "Oh, I see," she said calmly.

She was glad when Giulia went back to the kitchen, leaving her alone to finish her breakfast. Her head ached and her mouth felt dry and she was utterly miserable. The world was an unyielding and unsympathetic place and she knew that she couldn't put off telling her father about her marriage for very much longer. She couldn't even begin to imagine what his reaction would be! Nor could she think that it would be favourable. How could it be? His staid, practical daughter, whose one ambition had been to teach, abducted by a Sicilian and forced into marriage! It wasn't the kind of thing that *happened* to her father's acquaintances, or to anyone else she knew, come to that!

When she had finished her breakfast, she called Saro to her and set off up the garden to the cypress trees. It was a place she looked on as being her own, for she had never seen anyone else there. There she could sit and think to her heart's content and there would be none to disturb her.

She sat on the fallen log she had discovered there before and gazed down at the sea below her. Some sea-birds flew over the water, almost level with where she sat, their mocking call echoing her thoughts. Saro barked at something he had seen half-way down the cliff, but she ignored him. The sun beat down over her head, bleaching the colours from the scenery. To her, though, it was still perfection. If she could not find happiness here, then she would find it nowhere!

She was still sitting there when she heard the footsteps of someone coming towards her. She looked over her shoulder, frowning at the intrusion, and was surprised to see that it was Pearl.

"What are you doing here?" she asked her ungraciously.

Pearl collapsed in a heap beside her. "Giulia said you were up here, or rather she pointed in this direction when I said your name a few times. Even then she was quite nasty. *La Signora Verdecchio*—!"

Ruth blushed. "It does sound odd," she admitted.

"Odd! It sounds like Mario's aunt!" Pearl retorted. She looked at her sister curiously. "How does it feel?" she asked.

Ruth shook her head. "What are you going to Palermo for?" she countered.

Pearl pouted thoughtfully. "I see it's still 'Keep off the Grass'. Not that it's any of my business—"

"No, it isn't," Ruth agreed heartily.

"Actually," Pearl began, "I came along to have a talk with you. I figured it was about time somebody did!"

Ruth bit her lip. Why?"

"Let's call it sisterly affection—"

"Indeed?" Ruth put in dryly.

Pearl opened her blue eyes wide. "Truly!" she exclaimed. "I was cross before, but I'm not any longer!"

"You don't need to be," Ruth said wearily.

Pearl considered this. "No, that's true. But, Ruth, what are *you* going to do?"

Ruth looked at her young sister with some amusement. "What would you suggest?" she asked.

Pearl looked helpless. "I don't know. Mario isn't an easy person to manage. If you'd asked me before you came racing over to Sicily in a fit of righteous indignation, I'd have told you so! He doesn't allow people to walk out on him!"

"So he told me," Ruth affirmed.

Pearl gave her a look of unmixed respect. "What on earth did you say to him?"

Ruth shrugged. "I don't know."

"I don't understand you!" Pearl burst out. "Do you *want* to be a doormat all your life? He'll walk all over you!" She eyed Ruth thoughtfully. "I suppose you'd like that!" she added with an aggrieved air.

"I might," Ruth agreed, a little surprised at her own lack of shame.

"I never thought to hear you say it!" Pearl marvelled. "Darling, you really must pull yourself together! I feel so sad and guilty because it was I who got you into this. I'll just have to rescue you, whether you like it or not!"

Ruth lifted her chin forcefully. "Please don't!"

"But, Ruth—"

"I can manage my own affairs!" Ruth went on grimly.

"But that's just what you can't do!" Pearl exclaimed, exasperated. "You—you're positively *callow* when it comes to men!"

Ruth laughed helplessly. "Oh, Pearl! I'm not!"

"Well, you haven't my experienced approach!" Pearl sniffed.

"I should hope not!" said Ruth, her lips trembling with laughter.

"Well, you haven't! If you ask me, I think we'd better go back to England and the bosom of our loving family, and forget that we ever met Mario!"

"I can't!" Ruth said flatly.

"What else *can* you do?"

"Stay here."

"On your own?" Pearl looked dumbfounded. "He'd eat you up! Piecemeal!"

Ruth straightened her back and lifted her head. "I don't think he will," she said slowly. "You see, one of the advantages of being callow, in fact downright green, is that you don't break at all easily—"

"But he's only got to find out that you're in love with him!" Pearl protested.

"I'm not sure that I am," Ruth said with dignity.

Pearl's eyes grew round with astonishment. "What do you call it?" she asked.

Ruth bit her lip. "I don't know," she admitted. "But I'm not sure it's love. I'm not sure I even *like* him!"

"That's love!" said Pearl. "Believe me!" She giggled. "Oh, Ruth, you're such a fool! Did you really believe that it would give you a *cosy* feeling to fall in love?"

"No, of course not!" Ruth denied hastily.

"Well, anyway," Pearl went on with single-minded devotion to her own point of view, "whatever you call it, he's only got to find out about it and he's got you! You'd do far better to get away while you can!"

Ruth shook her head. "I'm married to him," she reminded Pearl. "I can't do anything else but stay here."

Pearl frowned. "I think last night went to your head!" she said frankly. "You sound exactly like Aunt Lucia!"

Ruth studied her sister with a quizzical expression. "Are you sure it didn't go to your head?" she suggested gently.

Pearl looked abashed. "Maybe, just a little bit," she admitted. "The thing is that I like kissing Mario. It was nothing against you." She took a deep breath. "I know I said I'd take him away from you, but I wouldn't! As a matter of fact, I probably wouldn't have come to Sicily with him in the end. He's a bit deep for me—"

"But he sent you your ticket!" Ruth exclaimed.

"But I hadn't used the ticket," Pearl explained. "I might have done, or I might not, I don't know! Mario is so beautifully handsome that it makes one feel good to be seen with him, but he's *deep*. I like to play around in the shallow end."

Ruth was shocked. "If Father could hear you—" she began.

"He'd call me an amoral baggage and lecture me a little," Pearl finished for her. "You're really very alike. That's exactly what you'd like to do, isn't it?"

Ruth could not deny it. "I can't understand it," she said at last.

"There's safety in numbers," Pearl defended herself.

"I'm beginning to think you *deserve* Mario! You're as archaic in your ideas as this horrid island!"

Ruth felt quite shattered by this vision of herself. Her head ached worse than ever and she wished Pearl would go away and leave her alone.

"I hardly think Father will agree with you," she said, rather wistfully.

Pearl smiled with smug satisfaction. "Hardly!" she said cheerfully. "But surely you aren't going to be fool enough to tell him?"

"I must," Ruth said simply. "He has to know! I can't stay here for ever without some kind of explanation!"

Pearl wrinkled up her forehead thoughtfully. "A suitably edited version of events will be best for both of us," she opined finally. "I'll get Mario to work on it."

"No, you won't. I'll tell Father myself!" Ruth insisted.

Pearl stood up, patting her hair back into position and brushing down her skirt. "Do what you like!" she said in exaggerated accents. "*I* intend to hide behind Mario's broad back myself, so you'd better not say anything about *my* affairs to Father, or you'll be sorry!"

With swinging hips, she walked back down the path towards the house, looking the picture of youthful innocence and unworldly bliss, and leaving her sister as cross as two sticks and with her head aching worse than ever.

Telephoning England was a complicated operation. Ruth stood for what seemed hours in the hall, waiting for her call to go through. The long delay did nothing for her courage. She quite simply couldn't imagine what she was going to say to her father at all, when the line burred and clicked and the familiar English double ring rang in her ear.

Her father's voice sounded as close as if he were in the next room.

"What's the matter?" he asked her. "Have you run out of money?"

This was a long-standing joke between them, for while Pearl never had enough money with her no matter where she went, Ruth had always budgeted with care and had never yet had to ask her father for money.

"Something like that," Ruth said in a shaky voice.

"Look, honey, is something the matter?"

"*No!* Dad, are you there? There's nothing the matter, only I got married. M—Mario is going to write to you, or something, but I wanted to tell you myself."

There was a long silence at the other end, then her father said, "Ruth, are you happy?"

"I—I think so."

"You only *think so?*"

Ruth licked her lips nervously. "He's a Sicilian. He's different from anyone I've ever known before. He takes some getting used to," she added on a desperate note.

To her surprise, her father laughed. "I shall be interested to meet him," he said cheerfully. "If he can put my staid daughter into a dither, he must be something!"

"Well, he is," Ruth answered judiciously.

Her father laughed again. "I'll tell your mother. But for heaven's sake write, Ruth! We shall want to hear all about him. And get that minx Pearl to come home, you'll hardly need her on your honeymoon!"

"I will," Ruth agreed mechanically. "I—I'll write today."

She said goodbye to her father with a rush of affection for him and the home he represented. It had always been a happy home. If she hadn't had much in common with her stepmother, they had always loved one another dearly, and they had laughed a lot. For a moment, she missed them all unbearably and would have given anything to have been going straight back to England and the comfortable *ordinariness* of her life there. But then the moment passed and she heard Henry's jeep in the drive and, a second later, he was standing at the front door with a slightly silly smile on his face.

"Hullo, Henry," she greeted him casually.

"Is Mario in?" he asked her cautiously.

Ruth shook her head. "Did you want him for anything special?" she asked.

Henry looked downright guilty. "Actually, I wanted to ask him if I could take Pearl round the vineyards," he explained. "I'm going to take a look at them now to see how the new irrigation is working."

"Then you can take me with you instead!" Ruth said firmly.

"I don't think I should," Henry said doubtfully. "I don't want to get in wrong with Mario."

"You won't!" Ruth assured him with a confidence she was far from feeling. "As a matter of fact both he and Pearl have gone in to Palermo and, as Lucia is with her husband, I'm the only person about."

"Oh," said Henry.

Ruth forced a laugh. "Don't look so hangdog!" she bade him briskly. "I've had a splitting headache all morning and it will do me good to get out and about for a while."

Henry muttered something about the hot sun and the lack of shade in the vineyards. "Besides," he added, "I don't know when we should be back, so he's bound to know."

"I don't care if he does!" Ruth insisted. "Oh, come on, Henry! What possible harm can there be in two English people going round some vineyards together? Just because *they* have medieval ideas about things, we don't have to do the same, surely?"

"No," Henry said bleakly. "Are you sure Pearl isn't here?" he pleaded.

"No, she's not!" Ruth snapped, much put out. "Are you going to take me or aren't you?"

"I suppose so," he said with a marked lack of enthusiasm. "You'd better bring a hat."

Such was Ruth's uncertain mood that as soon as she had persuaded him to take her she no longer wanted to go. She went reluctantly up to her room and stuck her hat on the top of her head with a marked lack of enthusiasm. When she went downstairs again Henry was already waiting for her in the jeep, looking just about as miserable as she felt.

"Do you know anything about vines?" she asked him.

"Not much." He sounded so woeful that she felt sorry for him and tried to pull herself together. As she had forced him to take her, the least she could do was to be a pleasant companion, she thought.

"I suppose they need a lot of water," she said brightly. "Was it Sicilian wine we had last night?"

"I should think it was a mixture of everything!" Henry grunted.

"Well, I thought it was very nice!" Ruth retorted.

Henry cheered up a trifle. "So did I! The Verdecchios mean a lot to the local people, don't they? I suppose they've had the same kind of do every time one of them has married for centuries past."

"Oh, do you think so?" Ruth asked, impressed.

"Setting the seal of ownership on their women," Henry added nastily.

Ruth tried to smile and failed. "I don't think that was kind, Henry," she reproached him.

"Well, I wish you hadn't made me take you with me! I have a horrid feeling that you're using me!"

"You're afraid of Mario!" Ruth taunted him.

"What if I am?" he demanded crossly. "Aren't you?"

"Certainly not!"

Ruth sat in a dignified silence while Henry drove rather fast down the drive and along the road to the village. The ground swept past far too quickly for her comfort and she grabbed at the windscreen for support in case they should swerve round a corner and she was thrown out.

They were already picking some of the grapes at the first vineyard they went to. The women did most of the actual picking, while the men gathered the bunches of grapes into baskets and transferred them to the carts that were drawn by patient horses.

"They look quite green!" Ruth exclaimed.

"They are green," Henry answered. "That's the main trouble with the wines from most of southern Italy. The grapes are picked far too early because they're always in a fright that they'll lose the crop to thieves, storm, or plague of some sort. They're often right too!"

"But *here*—?"

"Mario protects them, more or less," Henry granted magnanimously. "But the habit has taken root by now."

He stopped the jeep on the edge of the field and strode off down the lines of vines, pausing every now and again to examine the crop. Ruth followed him more slowly. The leaves of the vines smelt sweet and the grapes lay heavy, bowing down the more tender branches almost to the ground. There was no doubt that the irrigation scheme had been a success, for one could follow the path of the new water with one's eye, wherever the leaves were more verdant and the grapes bigger and juicier.

Some of the women stopped work and came across the fields towards her, excited by her unexpected visit. Their dark eyes watched her every movement, though they shied away whenever she returned their glances.

"We were there last night," one of them, braver than the rest, told her suddenly.

Ruth responded with a wide smile. "I want to thank you all for making it so beautiful for me," she said.

The women smiled. "Does the Signor know you are here?" they asked.

Ruth felt abashed. "Yes," she said uneasily.

Their smiles grew. "How pleased we are to see you!" they reiterated. "Are you hungry yet? Perhaps you would honour one of us by eating in the house?"

Ruth began to feel that she would. Mario could hardly object to her visiting other women, she thought. He might even be pleased that they appeared to like her and had asked her into their houses.

"But won't you be losing money if you stop work now?" she asked them.

They shrugged their shoulders. "The work will be here when we come back," they said philosophically.

With piercing tones, they informed the men where they were going, calling back and forth in sing-song voices as to which house they were going to and when they would be back.

They went to the house of a middle-aged woman which was quite near the vineyard. Her family, she told Ruth, had lived on Verdecchio land for generations past, and she herself wanted no other life.

"We have no difficulties here," she said darkly.

Everybody crowded into the small living room, in which the family cooked, ate, and some of them slept. A wooden chair was placed by the table for Ruth and the others sat where they could, the younger women standing in the doorway, pushing at one another, the better to see what was going on.

Ruth looked round the room expecting to see some signs of poverty she had been told she would find in Sicily, but there were none. The kitchen had an old-fashioned range of charcoal grates, in which fires were lit if there was any cooking to be done, with the aid of a fan, the *ciuscialoru*. Most of the utensils were old too and had probably been passed down from mother to daughter for generations. There were large copper cauldrons for boiling clothes, copper saucepans for boiling macaroni, a number of copper coffee pots of a Moorish design, and several other implements, all burnished and beautifully designed.

As well as the copper, there were the famous Sicilian water-jars, the *quartare*, which are made on the island of earthenware and are indispensable to most Sicilian households where the only water supply may be the fountain in the nearby square. These jars have the added advantage of cooling the water as well as storing it, for the water slowly permeates the coarse earthenware and the constant evaporation that results makes the water cool inside. In this kitchen there were two of these jars, as well as a number of other earthenware platters and dishes of various shapes and designs.

The woman of the house put wine and some local bread on the table.

"You will like our bread better than the bread from the continent," she told Ruth positively. "Sicilian bread is heavier and more salty!" She considered her guest for a moment. "Have you eaten our *pasta colle sarde* yet?"

Ruth was mystified, never having heard of such a dish.

"It is a treat!" all the women assured her. "Sophia

will cook it for you! It is a dish to tell your grand-children about!"

It was every bit as good as they said it was, Ruth decided, as Sophia heaped the mixture of macaroni, chopped sardines, pine nuts, fennel and raisins. She was a little afraid that she shouldn't accept so much from them, for only she was invited to partake of the dish, the rest of the women made do with large chunks of bread washed down with wine. But nor could she refuse. The best thing to do, she thought, was to enjoy every succulent mouthful of it, and then ask Mario afterwards how she could repay their hospitality.

The macaroni dish was followed by a *cassata siciliana*, a cake of magnificent proportions. It was round in shape, heavily iced and decorated with marzipan and sugared pieces. Inside it was flavoured with pistachio, cinnamon, chocolate, and probably a good many other things besides. Ruth found it delicious, even while she trembled at the number of calories each mouthful must have contained.

The women joined her in eating the cake. Sophia brewed some strong coffee and they sat on, sipping the hot beverage and gossiping until half the afternoon had gone by.

"Is the English Signor taking you home?" Sophia asked Ruth.

Ruth jumped guiltily. "I suppose so," she said.

"Then we had better take you back to him. He will be wanting to go on and you will be wanting to get home. Are you sure you have had enough coffee?"

"I've had heaps of everything!" Ruth confessed happily. "You are all very kind to me!"

"It is a pleasure to receive a visit from a Verdecchio," the women chorused dutifully.

They escorted her back along the road and across the vineyard to where Henry was waiting for her. He was cross and sticky from the hot sun and impatient to be gone as quickly as possible.

"With any luck Mario won't be back yet," he said sourly as she climbed into the jeep. "Though he's bound to hear about it from someone!"

"I don't see why he should mind," Ruth said stoutly.

"You don't want to see!" he told her flatly.

His nervousness was contagious. Ruth didn't enjoy the drive back to the house one bit. She went over all that she had said and done again and again, and, for the life of her, she couldn't see that she had done anything that Mario would not like—except to go with Henry in the first place!

"He took Pearl to Palermo," she said suddenly.

"What does that prove?" Henry retorted. "I wish I hadn't—" He broke off, his face aghast. "Oh no!" he gasped.

Ruth's eyes followed his to where Mario was standing, leaning negligently against one of the gate posts. He didn't even look up as the jeep approached, she noticed. He looked calm and confident, even placid, as he waited.

Henry slowed to a stop as they came level to the gates. He looked so guilty and nervous that Ruth was annoyed. She gave Mario a brilliant smile to show that she at least was not in the least afraid of him.

"Get out!" he said briefly.

Ruth stared at him. "Why should I?"

"Do you mean to say you don't know?" he mocked her. "Ask Henry!"

She clenched her fists angrily. "He didn't want to take me. I made him—" she began.

"That I can believe!" he answered sharply.

He reached into the jeep, hooked an arm under her, and deposited her none too gently on her feet beside him.

Henry looked more anxious than ever. "She spent her time with the women," he told Mario hastily.

"Then you needn't be further concerned," Mario answered with contempt. "If you go up to the house, Pearl is waiting for you."

Henry's face cleared as if by magic. "I'll do that!" he said eagerly. He put his foot down hard on the accelerator and the jeep sped away from them up the drive to the house.

"D-did Pearl like Palermo?" Ruth asked, taking the war firmly into the enemy's camp.

"I didn't ask her," Mario answered slowly. "Did Henry tell you that I told him not to take you gadding round with him in that jeep of his?" he added, almost casually.

She glanced up at him and away again. "Yes. But I couldn't see why—"

"No?" he cut her off. He looked very dangerous, she thought, and she despaired of ever explaining just why she had gone with Henry.

"You may have married me," she began grandly, "but that doesn't make me a Sicilian wife with nothing better to do than to seek the approval of her husband! I *enjoyed*—"

"Then I'll explain it to you," he said slowly. "You are married to me. You are a Sicilian wife, for I am a Sicilian, and so you'll live according to our ideas of what is permissible and what is not. And you have nothing better to do than to please me, and this is why!" He pulled her into his arms and kissed her so hard that she had no breath left with which to defy him. She made a little sound of protest, but then she could do nothing at all. For a moment, she stood stock still, shaken and more than a little frightened. *She would not kiss him back!* But she was a traitor to her own cause and with a little sob, she strained towards him, eager in her submission to the warmth of his lips and the unyielding strength of his arms.

When he let her go, her cheeks were scarlet and the tears started into her eyes. "I hate you! *I hate you!*" she stormed at him, stamping her foot.

He laughed, and pulled her back into his arms.

"So I see!" he said.

CHAPTER TEN

"THAT," she informed him roundly, "doesn't mean a thing!"

She took the opportunity of retreating a few paces away from him, shocked by the urgent desire within herself to fling herself back into his arms and tell him she would be pleased, *proud*, to do whatever he wanted of her.

"No?" He looked at her thoughtfully.

Ruth lifted her chin defiantly. "No!"

"Then you won't mind if I kiss you again?" he suggested smoothly.

He looked as if he would be as good as his word and Ruth backed away from him as hard as she could. He smiled at her and her heart turned right over.

"Well?" he said. "You might even kiss me?"

She gave him a quick, harassed look. "You don't understand!" she flared at him.

He took her hands back into his. "Explain it to me," he said, with such sympathy that she was sorely tempted to give way.

She shrugged her shoulders instead. "I can't!" she said. "It isn't *enough*!"

"It's a good deal," he pointed out with an amused grin.

"For *you*!" she stormed back. "You can come and go as you please! *Do* as you please! Why can't I?"

He was very gentle. "What do you want to do?" he asked her.

She saw, too late, that she had fallen into a trap

of her own making. There was only one thing she wanted to do and that was to creep back into his arms on any terms he cared to offer her. But she would not be so craven! She drew in a deep breath. "Does it matter?" she challenged him.

His eyes filled with warm laughter. "Not a bit," he replied swiftly, "if what you want to do is the same as what I want to do!" He looked so innocent that she was suspicious. "This, for example," he went on casually.

She felt that she knew then what any small animal felt when an eagle swooped down on it and carried it up into the sky. As his lips came down on hers, she shut her eyes. Her will-power skidded away from her and she was hazily aware that she was enjoying the fact.

When he released her, she swallowed hard, struggling to regain her equanimity.

"I suppose you kiss Pearl like that too!" she challenged him, aware that she was flirting with danger, but quite unable to resist the temptation.

His face hardened. "And what is that to you?"

She didn't answer. If she had, he would have known that she was consumed by jealousy for his interest in anyone else, and she would sooner have died than for him to know that! She didn't know when she had passed through such a shattering few minutes of self-revelation. If he kissed her *again*—! But already he had no excuse for not knowing that to her he was both ecstasy and the depths of despair. And she had thought of him as being a tiger! Why, the tiger was within herself and she had never even suspected its existence, she had been so busy being quiet and respectable and—and *dull*!

In a state of considerable agitation, she pulled herself free and ran away from him, as fast as she could, up the drive to the house and safety. Saro, the dog, welcomed her at the front door by barking his head off, and rushed up the stairs after her with yelps of delight at this new and unexpected game.

At the top of the stairs, Ruth crashed into Pearl without even seeing her.

"I thought you'd gone out with Henry!" she accosted her sister.

Pearl shrugged. "I didn't want to. Whatever happened to you?" she added curiously.

"I'm going home!" Ruth announced. "*Now*!"

"But I thought you were going to stay here for ever, waiting for the crumbs to fall?" Pearl reminded her, her blue eyes wide and innocent.

"Well, now I'm not!" Ruth retorted. The panic that had gripped her was beginning to subside, but she was still quite determined to run as fast and as far as she could.

"Good!" said Pearl. "And how are we going to leave?"

"I don't know," Ruth admitted. "But it must be possible. Did you buy your ticket when you were in Palermo?"

"*My* ticket, not yours! You haven't got a passport at the moment. Mario left it off at the British Consulate to have the name altered—"

"Oh no!" Ruth exclaimed wearily.

"I don't see that it matters," Pearl said reasonably. "If you're really determined to go, you can wait a few days, surely?"

"No, I can't!" Ruth snapped back. "I'll—I'll—" Her brow cleared dramatically. "I'll get Roberto to help me!" she said with relief, and blinked earnestly at her sister. "You won't breathe a word of this to Mario, will you?"

"I'm not a sneak!" Pearl denied, hurt. "I happen to

think that you won't lose Mario as easily as you think, but that's your affair."

The very mention of Mario gave Ruth a desperate feeling. "Pearl, you've got to help me! There isn't anyone else!"

"I've said I will," Pearl retorted with a touch of irritation. "Though I don't suppose you'll thank me when I have helped you. If you ask me, it will be a relief to everyone concerned when you and Mario sort yourselves out! He won't so much as look at *me* at the moment, and you seem to have lost your head entirely!"

This complaint brought an involuntary smile to Ruth's lips. "He took you to Palermo," she reminded her.

"So he did!" Pearl drawled. "What a thrill for me!"

"You would have thought so a few days ago," Ruth said bitterly.

"I might have done," Pearl agreed, striking a dramatic attitude of what she thought a romantic heroine ought to look like. "*That* was a few days ago. Strictly platonic relationships aren't in my line, though," she added.

"It doesn't look particularly platonic from where I'm sitting," Ruth told her grumpily. "Oh, Pearl, how can you say so! It *couldn't* have been platonic when he sent you the tickets to come to Sicily!"

"Love them and leave them, that's my motto!" Pearl answered with a touch of humour. "I don't think Mario agrees with me, somehow." She shivered slightly. "You know, Ruth dear, I don't envy you your Sicilian bandit! It *may* be my nice nature that refuses to envy any sister of mine, but I don't think so. I like being free and I like to enjoy myself. By the time Mario has finished with you, you won't be able to call your soul your own!"

"I know," Ruth said simply.

"So that isn't why you're rushing headlong in the opposite direction?" Pearl sighed.

"N-no," Ruth admitted.

"Then *why*?"

Ruth swallowed. "I can't explain!" she parried quickly. "It's all so awful! I never did understand about honour and so on. I suppose I gambled on it and I lost."

Pearl looked increasingly bewildered. "What on earth are you talking about?" she demanded. "You're in love with him, aren't you?" She barely waited for Ruth's faint nod of the head. "Well, there you are? What more do you want?"

"For him to be in love with me!" Ruth burst out. She coloured up finely. "N-not a grand passion," she defended herself immediately. "N-not m-much at all, but just a little bit!"

Pearl stared at her, feeling quite uncomfortable in the face of such intensity of emotion. "Goodness!" she said blankly.

"It isn't very flattering to mean nothing more than—than an honourable gesture!" Ruth went on, pursuing her point to the bitter end.

Pearl giggled. "Have you told him so?" she asked.

"No." Ruth looked the very picture of dejection. "You must see that I *couldn't*!"

"Well, I think he's guessed!" Pearl said coolly. "He's no fool, and anybody can see that there's something the matter with you! When I think about how you lectured me! And I've never done anything as awful as allowing any man to capture me like some—some Sabine woman!"

"Some *what*?" Ruth gasped.

Pearl creased up her forehead. "Perhaps they weren't Sabines," she said thoughtfully. "But they didn't want to go back to their own men when they were

rescued. They preferred to stay with the Romans!"
she finished triumphantly, pleased to be able to
produce this piece of classical history from some
distant Latin class. "You must know the story, Ruth.
It was about the only interesting one in the book."

Ruth sat stock still, her back as stiff as a poker.
"Are you suggesting," she asked awfully, "that I
don't really want to go home?"

"No," Pearl said pacifically. "But I don't think
you'd want to go if you weren't pretty sure that
Mario will come after you." She eyed her sister
thoughtfully. "Don't blame me, that's all, if you get
hurt!"

"I won't!" Ruth said dourly.

"That's all right, then," Pearl said with grudging
approval. "You'd better set about getting Roberto to
retrieve your passport for you. I shall hitch a ride
into Palermo and get you a ticket. Have you got any
money?"

Ruth found her purse and opened it. At first sight
it looked as if she had millions of *lire*, but when she
counted them up they didn't look as they were going
very far.

"Will you have enough, do you think?" she asked
Pearl anxiously.

Pearl accepted the bundle of notes with a resigned
expression. "It won't allow for luxuries, will it?" she
said sourly. "What have you done with all the
money we brought with us?"

"I left it at the hotel in Naples for you," Ruth
said.

Pearl looked a trifle guilty. "Oh, was I supposed to
keep it?" she muttered. "I thought it was something
to keep me entertained while you were away."

"Oh, Pearl, you didn't! What on earth did you
spend it on?"

"Shoes mostly," Pearl remembered with glee. "Italian shoes must be the best in the world! I've never seen such gorgeous, fragile creations! I could have bought up the whole shop!"

"But they weigh so heavily," Ruth protested feebly. "What are you going to do on the flight home?"

"Smile at the man who weighs us in," Pearl said simply.

Feeling more than a little harassed, Ruth went downstairs again, hoping to find Roberto on his own. In this she was lucky, for Mario's uncle had deposited his wife at the house of some friends and had come home himself, looking for a quiet place where he could have a smoke and read some papers to do with his business. It had been a bad time for him to come away from Tunis, pleased as he had been to snatch a few days in his native Sicily, and he felt obliged to carry on with as much work as he could while he was there.

He looked up from the gilded sofa on which he was seated as Ruth came into the room.

"Ah, my dear, how nice! Have you come to have a chat with me?" His eyes noted her goaded expression with something very like amusement. "You know that I am very much at your service."

"Thank you," she said with dignity. She sat down quickly on a small chair, facing him, wondering how she could possibly make her request known to him. If only he had looked a little less like Mario!

"It's something dreadful!" she confessed in a forlorn voice.

"But not so dreadful that it can't be put right?" he suggested.

She took courage from his quiet confidence and relaxed a trifle. "Will you help me?" she asked him frankly.

"That's what I came to Sicily to do," he reminded her quietly.

"Yes, I know," she said, and stopped. She looked at him earnestly. "I can't stay here after all!" she explained in a little burst. "I thought I could, but I can't!"

She more than half expected his expression to harden as Mario's did whenever he was crossed, but Roberto remained perfectly calm. "Then of course nobody will make you stay," he said quietly.

"But that's just it! Mario took my passport in to Palermo and now I don't know if I even have one! And Pearl has bought shoes with most of the money! And our return tickets only go from Naples, and I don't know if we have enough to get there! And even if we could, I can't go *anywhere* without a passport!"

He seemed to have no difficulty in sorting out this rather garbled account. "I suppose your passport is at the British Consulate? But that's the easiest thing in the world! We shall call there and ask them for it. They can hardly refuse to give it to you."

"But Mario may—"

"I hardly think that even Mario has found a way to subvert the entire British diplomatic corps to his own ends," Roberto said dryly.

Ruth perceived that she was being silly. She blushed to the roots of her hair. "N-no," she agreed.

"Nor does your being married to him mean that you automatically lose your British status," Roberto reassured her. As this was not a contingency that had previously occurred to Ruth, she was far from being grateful for this piece of information.

"I *won't* be Sicilian!" she stormed at him.

Roberto grinned at her. "Italian," he said.

"I don't care what you call it, I won't be it!" Ruth said sulkily. The prospect of having her nationality snatched away from her began to loom large in her mind. "It's just the sort of thing Mario would do to me!"

Roberto looked intrigued. "Do you think so?" he asked gently.

Ruth bit her lip. She gave a reluctant laugh and promptly felt very much better. "I'm sorry!" she said impulsively. "I can't think what's the matter with me, I'm so jumpy! And you're being so kind too! Do you really think you can get my passport back?"

"I shall be very surprised if I don't." He patted her hand encouragingly. "There's no need to look like that, my dear. If you want to leave Sicily, you shall, and nobody will stop you—not even Mario!"

A new anxiety occurred to Ruth. "You won't tell him, will you?" she demanded. "I—I couldn't bear him to know!"

"He will have to know some time," Roberto pointed out.

"But he won't let me go! He'll stop me, I know he will!"

He began to think it was only too likely. If Ruth was able to work herself up into such a state at the mere thought of his nephew, he was inclined to think that Mario had only to appear over her horizon for her to become completely hysterical. As he was not particularly enamoured of having to deal with hysterical females, no matter how fond he was of them in their calmer moments, he promised himself a few well-chosen words with his nephew at the first opportunity that presented itself. Meanwhile, he reluctantly returned his attention to Ruth.

"There is absolutely nothing for you to worry about," he reiterated firmly. "If you will go and pack your things, I will have the car sent round and will take you to Palermo myself."

Ruth sighed with relief. "You're being very kind to me," she said gratefully.

He looked amused. "The Verdecchios have a weakness for helping pretty girls," he teased her.

She was inordinately pleased. "I'm not really pretty," she denied. "But it's nice to be told that you are!"

"What makes you think you are not pretty?" he asked with interest.

"Pearl is pretty," she said seriously. "I don't pretend to compete with her!"

"I imagine you don't have to," he answered gallantly. "She has a pretty face and taking ways. You have something else—"

Ruth looked at him inquiringly, fascinated. "What else?" she asked.

He considered her. "Zest," he said promptly. "I don't think your spirits fail you often, and that's a far more lasting quality than mere prettiness."

She didn't know whether to be pleased or sorry by his analysis.

"It isn't very spirited to run away, is it?" she said humbly.

His eyes twinkled. "I don't know," he said frankly. "Only you can answer that."

"Then I think it's the bravest thing I've ever done in my life!" she said flatly, and gave him an uncertain smile. "Do you think me very silly?"

His own smile answered her. "You're a woman," he said, as if that were answer enough. "And I daresay your instinct is as sound as most!"

She could only hope he was right.

Pearl was glad to be going. She got into the car without a backward look at the chauffeur who was struggling to lift her suitcase into the boot beside Ruth's.

"It will be nice to see England again" she yawned. "Italy is really a very disappointing place."

Ruth leaped headlong to Italy's defence! "In what way?" she demanded. "I find it lovely! Where else have you ever been where you can smell the lemons growing on the trees? I think it's beautiful! You should have seen the inside of their houses! The copper pans and implements are things of beauty in their own right. *They* don't cook with mass-produced pots and pans and stainless steel and endless quantities of convenience foods!"

"Nobody's making you come away," Pearl reminded her smugly.

Ruth lapsed into silence. It was harder to leave Sicily than she had imagined. She had wept a little when she had said goodbye to Saro, shutting him into the stables so that he wouldn't run after her. It was a funny thing, but she had felt at home from the moment she had stepped off the boat. None of the island had come as a surprise to her; it was almost as if it had always been a part of her, waiting somewhere in her subconscious to be recognised. The brilliant contrasts between light and shade, the cobbled squares, the fountains, the vineyards and, perhaps, particularly, the masses of colourful flowers that grew everywhere, even on the crowded balconies. In a few days, it had become more her home than the green, flowing fields of England, and the grey stone buildings of the school where she had taught. Where she still did teach, she corrected herself gloomily. She sniffed, making a brave attempt not to feel sorry for herself.

Roberto got into the front seat beside the chauffeur. He was wearing dark glasses which gave him a mysterious look. He didn't even turn round to look at the two girls, but nodded to the chauffeur to drive on.

"First, the British Consulate," he murmured. "Then we shall see."

The road flashed by all too quickly. Ruth peeped out of the car as they came to the gates to see if Mario was still there, but there was no sign of him. A sob broke in the back of her throat and the tears poured silently down her cheeks. She would never see him again! And she *hated teaching*!

Pearl handed her a handkerchief and frowned at her. "For heaven's sake—" she began, much put out.

"I fancy she is better left alone," Roberto said from the front seat.

Pearl shrugged. "I think she's barmy!"

Roberto smiled wearily. "Only unhappy, I think," he said.

Ruth was grateful for his forbearance. She blinked the tears out of her eyes so that she could see her last of Sicily, trying hard to pull herself together. She owed it to Pearl to be something better than a tearful wreck, she thought. These last few days had been hard for her too. Ruth remembered how hard it had been to persuade her to come to Italy with her at all.

"A lot of classical ruins!" she had said. "Why on earth do you want to go and stare at them?"

"I teach people about them," Ruth had reminded her.

Pearl had made a face at her. "I prefer the living to the dead!" she had said grandly. "You can't live your life with a ruin!"

The tears came storming back into Ruth's eyes. How right she had been! It had seemed so important

to her though, to wander through Italy, re-living
the history of a different people in a different age.
She must have been mad! For what pillar, or ancient stone, could compare with Mario's little finger,
or even with Saro? The thought of the little dog was
too much for her and she blew her nose with determination.

The car stopped outside the British Consulate
while Roberto got out.

"Perhaps you had better wait somewhere," he suggested vaguely. 'The *café piccola*. I'll meet you there
as soon as I have your passport."

The chauffeur drove away a few yards down the
street and came to a stop again beside a small café
that spilled out over the pavement, a huddle of
highly coloured tables and chairs, half hiding behind
a wooden lattice screen over which a creeper
climbed, a mass of heavy, hanging trumpet flowers,
beneath which swirled the dust from the street.

Ruth and Pearl sat outside at one of the tables
while the chauffeur went inside to buy himself a
glass of brandy. A waiter came out and took their
order for coffee and the delicious ice cream that
Italy is renowned for.

"I can't think what Father is going to say!" Pearl
said in matter-of-fact tones as the coffee arrived.
"What will you do if he says you ought to come
back?"

Ruth shook her head. "He won't," she said.

"Perhaps not to you!" Pearl admitted. "It would
be a different story if it were me! I wonder why he
thinks you're so level-headed and me such a will-o'-
the-wisp? He must be a very bad judge of character!"

Ruth tried to smile. "I always have been level-
headed," she protested.

Pearl gave a brittle laugh. "Until now!" she agreed. She watched Ruth wince and her eyes opened innocently. "It will be interesting to see how Father responds to his new daughter—"

"Don't, Pearl!" Ruth pleaded.

But Pearl was enjoying herself. "He thinks I'm a baggage! Imagine what he'll call you when he finds out that you're besotted with a man like Mario who doesn't give a rap for you!"

"He married me," Ruth said through clenched teeth.

Pearl sucked at her ice-cream spoon with ill-concealed triumph. "But it hardly looks as if you are going to *stay* married to him! Despite all your high moral principles and submissive ways!" She frowned and then smiled. "Oh, don't listen to me, Ruth. You know I don't mean it!"

Ruth didn't answer. She ate her ice-cream mechanically and sipped at her coffee. She wasn't even listening to what Pearl was saying. She was too busy fighting the grey despair that threatened to completely engulf her. Was she mad to refuse what Mario cared to offer her because she couldn't have everything she wanted? She really didn't know.

Roberto joined them just as they were finishing their coffees. He waved the passport in triumph, throwing it down on the table beside Ruth.

"They did it while I waited," he told her. "You have to sign it somewhere before you can use it."

Ruth opened it timidly. Only the picture of herself was familiar. She couldn't imagine where it had come from, but it was certainly a good likeness, a much better likeness than she had had in her passport before. Otherwise, everything in it was strange and unfamiliar. *Signora Verdecchio*, she read with dismay, followed by her Christian names, Ruth Anne. She wasn't even herself any more!

Luckily, she was not allowed to brood on her change of identity. Roberto hurried them away from the café.

"We shall be late for the boat for Naples unless we hurry," he told them. "We still have Ruth's ticket to get. We have no time to linger!"

It was something new to Ruth to have a man to manage her affairs for her. It was rather pleasant, she discovered, to have Roberto to buy her ticket for her and to find a porter to take the luggage on board, while she had nothing to do but to stand beside the gangway until it was time to go up it as the ship was sailing. It showed no signs of doing so, however, and most of the crew were still lounging on the deck, watching the world go by below them.

Ruth lost interest in the doings of her own ship as another boat started to come in alongside. Standing on the deck, obviously hoping to be the first ashore, stood the most lovely woman that Ruth had ever seen. She was no longer young, but even from a distance she was able to see beautiful planes of her face and the sweet expression that flickered across her face, mixed with an impatience at the delays in letting down the gangway.

Roberto came up beside Ruth and handed her her ticket.

"I must pay you," she said, and began to search in her handbag, forgetting that she had given all the money to Pearl.

"No, no," he argued. "We owe you this much, no? It is a small thing, my dear. A very small thing."

She sensed that any further argument would be distasteful to him, so she thanked him warmly instead, reaching up and kissing him on the cheek.

"Have you ever seen anyone lovelier than that woman over there?" she asked him, changing the subject quickly to hide her embarrassment, for there was no doubt about it, he did look very like Mario.

Roberto turned to look where she was pointing. His serious face broke into smiles and he began to run towards the boat.

"Mary-Anne! Mary-Anne!"

The woman searched the crowd, looking for the person who was calling her name, a half-smile just touching her lips.

"Roberto!" she called back. "Oh, Roberto, you don't know how pleased I am to see you! I couldn't stay in New York a minute longer! I had to see her for myself!"

The gangway clattered down on to the quay and the woman flung herself down it, abandoning her luggage to the goodwill of her fellow passengers. She embraced Roberto with warm affection. "Do you mind?" she asked him guiltily. "How is Lucia?"

"We are all delighted that you have come," he responded happily. "Yes, I think you will like her, but she is determined to go back to England. And Lucia is very well."

Mary-Anne's startled expression made Ruth want to smile.

"Back to England?" Mario's mother repeated. "But I've only just come!"

"You didn't let us know—" Roberto fussed, but Mary-Anne's attention had already left him. She looked about her, the determined look in her eye reminding Ruth of Mario at his most arrogant. It was intolerable that it should be so, but she felt a rush of affection for Mary-Anne because of it. Their eyes met and Mario's mother smiled at her.

"I think you must be Ruth?" she said diffidently. "You are so exactly what I would have chosen for my son!" She turned back to Roberto. "Where is Mario?"

"At home," he told her.

"Then we must go there at once!" She cast a displeased look at the sisters' luggage and the porter who was struggling to carry it up the gangway. "And I won't hear another word about anyone going to England!" She smiled slowly at Ruth. "Sicily is always home to us Sicilian wives—worse luck!" she added wryly. "Even in New York!"

CHAPTER ELEVEN

"EVEN if you are staying, I am going home," Pearl said evenly. "I feel decidedly *de trop* amongst your new relations—"

Mary-Anne regarded her quizzically. "I imagine that you might," she agreed. "I'm surprised you didn't go before."

Ruth felt distinctly uncomfortable. None of them were being fair to Pearl! But they needn't think that they could dismiss any sister of hers so easily! She would see to that!

"Pearl has been a very welcome guest of both Mario and myself!" she addressed her mother-in-law haughtily.

Mary-Anne raised a thoughtful eyebrow. "Really?" she drawled.

Ruth remembered the row she had had with Mario over Pearl's visit and blushed. "If it hadn't been for Pearl then I never would have married Mario," she went on doggedly.

"Now that I can believe!" Mary-Anne said warmly. "But one can't have one's sister around one for ever, can one?"

Ruth, who at any other time would have been glad to see Pearl go, shook her head. "Mario likes her," she said. She gave Roberto a look of mute appeal to help her, but he too seemed to have nothing better to do than to speed Pearl on her way.

"She must do as she pleases, of course!" he ended a rather garbled piece of advice to the effect that Pearl would have to pay heavily if she didn't use her ticket back to England.

"And I choose to go home!" Pearl reiterated. "Sicily is *not* for me! If you had any sense, Ruth, you'd come with me!"

Ruth smiled fainly. "I know," she said. "Oh, Pearl! I don't know what to do!"

Pearl gave her a quick hug. "You won't be coming home," she told her frankly. "We both knew that all the time! Goodness knows why you have to drive yourself to the point of despair! I don't! I settle for what I can get—"

"But *I can't*!" Ruth exclaimed helplessly.

"Then come with me," Pearl retorted, not without humour. "Only, for heaven's sake, make up your mind, or the boat will go without either of us!"

Ruth didn't know what she might have decided. She hesitated, wishing for the first time in her life that she didn't have to make the decision. She felt foolish and feminine and rather weak-kneed. If only someone would tell her what to do! But there was no one. Mary-Anne and Roberto were busy talking to one another and Pearl was engaged in separating her luggage from Ruth's and instructing the porter to carry only that on board the ship. Ruth felt both ignored and lonely. Nobody really cared, she thought, what she did!

Her eyes filled with tears that she tried her best to blink away. She turned her head and watched fascinated as a small dog raced across the quay towards her, scattering ruin as he came. Luggage was overturned, women were tripped up, and children knocked flat, but Saro didn't care a rap for any of them. He gave a final leap into Ruth's arms, barking uproariously an exuberant greeting.

"Oh, Saro!" she sobbed against his neck. "How did you get here?"

An argument swiftly followed the dog's arrival. Angry people gathered round Ruth and the dog, prodding her with angry fingers and shouting at her with even more angry voices.

"I don't understand what you're saying!" she told them frantically in English.

The uproar began again and stopped only with the arrival of a policeman, who shouted as much and as often as everyone else.

"Is this your dog?" he asked Ruth eventually.

"Well—" she began.

"He belongs to you?" the policeman insisted.

Ruth looked over the policeman's shoulder straight into Mario's dark eyes. She clutched Saro closer to her, feeling more and more harassed.

"N-not exactly," she said.

Mario strolled through the crowd to her side. "It's very unwise not to tell the police the truth," he observed gravely.

Ruth gave him a look of unspeakable loathing. "I am telling the truth!" she said heatedly.

The policeman was relieved to see one calm man in the crowd around him. He addressed Mario eagerly, with a wide, flattering smile. "This dog is not under proper control. You can see for yourself that it has inconvenienced many people already—"

Mario's eyes twinkled. "He certainly has!" he agreed warmly.

The policeman sighed. "Can you tell me, *signore*? To whom does the dog belong?"

"To my wife," Mario replied promptly.

The policeman looked startled. "But this young lady is travelling to Naples?" He glanced down at Ruth's luggage. "She has English labels, *signore*," he said suspiciously.

"I *am* English," Ruth put in gently.

"Then the dog does not belong to you?"

Ruth hesitated. She tucked Saro under her arm,

feeling a traitor for denying the bond between them. "Not really. I mean——"

"She means that the dog was a wedding present to her," Mario interrupted helpfully.

"He belongs to the Verdecchio family," Ruth added firmly.

The policeman cast his attention back to her. "And your name, *signora*?"

"Ruth Arnold——"

"Signora Verdecchio!" Mario answered as well, thoroughly enjoying himself.

The policeman threw up his hands in despair. "I must see your passport!" He took the document from Ruth's reluctant hand. "Signora Verdecchio!" he confirmed, and gave Ruth the respectful look one might accord a lunatic. "Perhaps you have not been married very long? But I must ask you to keep your pet under control, *signora*! The world goes on!" He grinned at Mario and bowed. "Many years of happiness to you both!"

Mario shook hands with him. When he wanted, Ruth thought bitterly, he had quite the common touch. He didn't have to be arrogant and devilish and impossible! So why did he have to be like that with her?

"Did you think you would escape so easily, *piccina*?" he asked her when the policeman had gone.

"You should have let me go," she answered evenly. "It isn't as if you care!"

"I care very much that my wife——"

"But I'm *me*!" Ruth said sharply.

He looked amused. "So I see," he said.

Ruth blushed. "Your mother's here!" she blurted out, determined to distract his attention.

She was touched by the quick look of affection that crossed his face, even though he turned away from her. He really loved his mother, she thought. Well, there was no surprise in that! Ruth thought she could quite easily love her herself, if only for a certain look in her eye that was so strangely like her son's.

Mary-Anne took a step forward and her son took her into his arms.

"*Mamma mia!*" he said in her ear. "Have you come home?"

Mary-Anne sniffed and nodded. "For always!" she said with a touch of exasperation. "New York isn't home to me any more! Oh, Mario, will you mind having me here?"

His dark face grew very gentle. "It wasn't I who wanted you to go away," he reminded her.

She gave a wavery laugh. "No, but I was lonely here without Papa. Only I was more lonely in New York!"

He kissed the end of her nose. "It will be less lonely, Mamma, for now you will have Ruth—"

"But she's going to England! Didn't you know?"

"No, no," he assured her. "Ruth came to see her sister off!"

Mary-Anne didn't argue with him. Instead she patted his shoulder comfortably and smiled mistily up at him. "Do I look awful?" she asked him. "I was determined that I wouldn't cry! I hate crying! I always feel so awful afterwards!"

He grinned. "If you call that crying—! Mamma—"

"What do you call it?" she demanded crossly.

"Wasting an elegant tear," he teased her. "Mamma darling, you cry as beautifully as you do everything else, so you have nothing to worry about! Ask Ruth, if you don't believe me!"

Mary-Anne obediently turned to her daughter-in-law. "It's so nice to be home!" she exclaimed. She gave Ruth a rueful smile. "You must think me very interfering," she sighed. "And I *promised* myself that I would be nothing of the sort! I didn't mean to be rude to your sister, my dear."

Mario smiled at them both. "Where *is* Pearl?" he asked.

Ruth looked up at the ship where Pearl's ash-blonde hair was easy to be seen. "She's gone on board," she said. "She doesn't want to stay any longer."

Mario looked at her keenly. "Do you mind so much?" he asked.

Ruth shook her head, unable to lie about it. "No," she said abruptly.

Mary-Anne went limp with relief. "I'm sure she will be much happier amongst her own friends," she said politely.

Ruth gave Mario a cross look. "I don't know why you have to be so beastly about her! Just because Pearl isn't—doesn't *pretend* to think that everything Sicilian is the best in the world—"

"*What*?" Mario gasped.

"She doesn't happen to admire men who think they're the lords of the earth! I'm not sure that I do either!"

"Only not sure?" he inquired demurely.

"*Quite* sure!"

Mary-Anne laughed at them both. "Children! Hadn't you better wave Pearl goodbye?"

Ruth was furious with herself. How could she have stood there bickering with Mario while Pearl sailed away? She rushed to the edge of the quay as the ship pulled away out into the centre of the harbour.

"Pearl!" she shouted out. "Tell the family—"

"I'll tell them," Pearl answered.

"I'm sorry I'm not coming with you!" Ruth called out pathetically.

Her sister laughed ungraciously. "I'll believe that when I see you in England!"

"But I'll miss you !"

Pearl's laughter grated on Ruth's ears. "Why pretend?" Pearl turned on her. "You're as glad to see the back of me as I am to be going! Oh, don't look so stricken! How I loathe intense people! Goodbye, Ruth!"

Ruth waved her hand, wishing that things between Pearl and herself could have been different. "Goodbye," she said.

The hooter blared above her head and the ship eased slowly out of her berth, taking Pearl out of sight and hearing. Ruth waved again and was dizzily happy when Pearl waved back. She should have known, she thought. Pearl never meant more than half of what she said.

Mario eased Saro away from her tight clasp. "Come on," he said gently. "It's time to go home."

Ruth wanted to travel back with Roberto. Mary-Anne would want to be alone with her son, she reasoned, and she would be glad to have a few minutes to herself to collect her scattered wits and to make some kind of decision about what she was going to do next.

Mario though had other ideas. The touch of his hand round her wrist was relaxed and gentle, but she knew better than to think that he wouldn't use physical force if he wanted to. In the end they would all travel home in the cars that he decided they would go in, so it hardly seemed worthwhile to have yet another battle of wills with him. It would be so much easier to surrender, she thought. She was tired and it hurt her badly every time she crossed swords with him.

Mario studied her face for a long moment. "You shouldn't have left Saro howling for you in the stables," he said gently.

"Is that how you knew I'd gone?" she demanded.

He nodded. "That and the fact that Sophia saw the car go by."

"And she *told you*?"

His dark eyes met hers. "She is one of my people," he answered simply. "Besides, she knows you are my wife!"

"Then she knows more than I do!" Ruth snapped back before she had thought.

"*And*," Mario went on just as if she hadn't spoken, "the place of my wife is by my side—"

"But your mother—"

Mario's patience snapped. He said something in an undertone to his uncle and towed Ruth away with him, whether she wanted to go or not. When they reached the car, he let her go and opened the door. "Get in!" he said briefly.

"But—" Ruth began.

"*Get in!*" he said again.

Ruth got in quickly and took Saro on her knee before Mario could touch her again. She was suddenly very glad to be in his car and to have him drive her home, but not for worlds would she have admitted the fact.

"Your mother is beautiful too," she said dreamily, as he got in the car beside her.

"More comparisons?" he asked, smiling.

"No," she said. "But she *is* beautiful."

"Yes, she is," he agreed. "Are you going to be jealous of her too?"

Ruth's lips twitched. "Certainly not!" she said with aplomb. "I think she's unhappy as well as beautiful," she added hesitantly.

"That's acute of you," he admitted. "Since my father died she has been unable to settle anywhere. I'm glad she's decided to come home, though, a few grandchildren will be a new interest for her."

Ruth's cheeks flamed. "I'm not sure—" she began.

He cast his amused eyes over her face. "Some time we'll talk about it," he said. "When we can be alone and sure that there won't be any interruptions."

"You mean you'll talk and I'll listen," she said in despair.

He laughed a great deal at that. "My dear girl, if you think I have any control over that ready tongue of yours—"

"But you don't listen to me!" she complained.

"Don't I?" His voice sounded so loving that she was obliged to swallow hard.

"You know you don't!" she said.

He started up the car with a flourish and laughed. "You shouldn't make it so tempting to *stop your mouth with kisses*!" he teased her, and waited with obvious delight for the colour to flood into her cheeks. "And hold that dog still! He has as little idea of how to behave in a car as he has in the house!"

Ruth held on to the dog tightly. "But then in your opinion neither of us know our place!" she reminded him smugly.

The glint in his eye made him look more devilish than ever. "It's something you can both be taught!" he answered her grimly.

She lifted her chin and glared at him. "You can try!" she challenged him.

He forbore to answer, but drove the car very fast out of Palermo and along the road towards his home. Ruth could feel the power of the car in the small of her back and found it a very satisfactory sensation.

"I shall want a car of my own," she informed him suddenly.

"You shall have one."

That caught her off balance. "When?" she asked cautiously.

"As soon as I can be sure that you won't rush off again!"

She sighed. "As soon as I know my place, in fact?"

He smiled. "No, there are other rewards for being good," he remarked.

She knew better than to ask him what they were. She thought she could imagine what he meant. Supposing, just supposing—She drew her thoughts up with a jerk. How could she actually want him to kiss her when he didn't love her! She wasn't the beautiful kind, such as the women he was accustomed to, so why should he look twice at her. She was his *wife*, family, someone to grow accustomed to, but not someone to love to distraction or until it hurt. And yet she would be content with such a small piece of his love, she told herself, and knew, even then, that it wasn't the truth. She wanted as much as she was prepared to give, and that was everything!

Lucia was waiting for them when they arrived at the house. She was so terribly relieved to see Ruth getting out of the car that Ruth wanted to laugh.

"Mario would have been sure to have blamed Roberto," Lucia said to Ruth. "And he would have been right! Nobody should come between a man and his wife!"

Ruth blinked. "Roberto was no more than kind to me," she answered with dignity.

"Yes, he is kind, isn't he?" Lucia agreed, much pleased. "I love him dearly because of it! But I'm also very glad you changed your mind and didn't go with Pearl. Mario is not always very kind and that can be very uncomfortable to bear with, let me tell you!"

She saw the second car draw up with Roberto and Mary-Anne in it and stood stock still with sheer surprise. A second later she had rushed forward and had pulled open the car door and was lavishly hugging her sister-in-law. "How could you come and not tell me?" she demanded. "Did Roberto know? How long do you stay? We have to be back in Tunis almost immediately, so it is fortunate we are here to see you! How mean of you not to give us any warning!"

"Yes, wasn't it?" Mary-Anne said, returning Lucia's hug with energy. "But I had to see my new daughter-in-law for myself!"

Lucia frowned. "But you made Roberto come from Tunis—"

Mary-Anne gave her a guilty smile. "I know I did. You see I was worried about her. I know what it feels like to be a brand-new wife, married to a Sicilian!"

Lucia giggled. "How could it feel but very nice?" she protested. "I remember your wedding very well, Mary-Anne, and *nothing* would have dragged you away from Sicily!"

"No, but I did feel lost. The more I thought about it the more I wanted to come and make it easier for Ruth."

Lucia, Sicilian born and bred, dismissed this as a peculiar foreign quirk. "Ruth is very well!" she said. "What could she possibly find wrong with being married to Mario?"

Mary-Anne made a face, hoping to silence her impulsive sister-in-law. "We'll have a nice gossip in a minute," she said. "But first I want to get to know my new daughter!"

Ruth, who had been standing tongue-tied while this conversation had been going on, found herself suddenly being grasped by her mother-in-law's hand and whisked into the house.

"You don't have to tell me, you have my old room!" Mary-Anne said gaily, running lightly up the stairs.

"D-do you mind?" Ruth answered, embarrassed. "I can easily move. I can use the room Pearl had—"

"Mario would be furious if you did!" Mary-Anne answered frankly. "No, my dear, any room will do for me tonight. I'll fix it up with Giulia if you don't mind, when we go downstairs again. I'm not sure that I want to live in this house anyway. I think I'll have a house of my own close by."

Ruth looked concerned. "I don't think Mario would like—" she began.

"I don't suppose he will," his mother agreed. "All Sicilians take their family responsibilities very seriously indeed. Still, I think if he sees that it's what I really want, he'll let me have it. He always does!"

Ruth had no confidence that Mario would prove so obliging about anything.

"It—it isn't because of me, is it?" she asked.

Mary-Anne looked at her with warm affection. "Not entirely. It's mostly because although I was married to a Sicilian, I still have American ideas about privacy and so on. I don't want to have people on top of me all day long, and I don't want to be on top of them either!"

"I'd love to have you here!" Ruth burst out.

Mary-Anne gave her a curious look. "To please Mario? Ruth honey, are you afraid of Mario in any way?"

Ruth shook her head. "Of course not!" she denied.

Mary-Anne was far from being convinced. "You can tell me, you know," she said, "because I shan't tell Mario—"

"I wouldn't care if you did!" Ruth assured her defiantly.

Mary-Anne giggled. "I expect it's your courage that made Mario want to marry you in the first place! Nothing appeals to him more!"

Ruth allowed her mother-in-law to precede her into her bedroom. Her defences had been sadly undermined by Mary-Anne's charming interest in her and she was in two minds as to whether she wouldn't be wise to tell her the whole story.

"It was a matter of honour," she said obscurely.

Mary-Anne looked at her with expectant interest. "I thought it might be when Lucia told me that it was a dark secret why you had got married. She seemed to think she had had quite a lot to do with bringing the two of you together."

"Only because she never came when she said she would!" Ruth remembered with a deep feeling of injury.

"Leaving you alone with Mario?"

Ruth nodded. "Only he wasn't here either—not really!"

Mary-Anne gave her a sympathetic look. "But I don't see what *you* were doing here?" she said gently.

Ruth blushed. "I came instead of Pearl—"

"Oh, I see!" Mary-Anne exclaimed.

"Do you?" Ruth said dubiously.

Mary-Anne pursed up her lips, her eyes laughing. "Of course! If Mario walked in and found *you* when he was expecting to find your sister, *of course* he wasn't going to let you go!"

Ruth was completely shaken by such an idea. She gave her mother-in-law a look of mute appeal and stuttered out something about it not having been quite like that!

Happily for Ruth's peace of mind, Lucia came upstairs carrying one of Mary-Anne's suitcases. "Which room shall I put it in?" she asked.

Mary-Anne looked at Ruth with perfect dignity. "Did you say I could have the one your sister had?"

"Yes—no—but—" Ruth gave the two older women a helpless look. "I th-think you should have the best room!" she managed finally to get out.

"Yes," Lucia agreed with a bounce that betrayed her sheer good spirits. "The one next to ours! I shall put your suitcase in there."

"And I'll tell Giulia to make up the bed," Ruth added quickly, taking her cue from them. It gave her a very good excuse to make her escape from the questioning eyes of Mary-Anne before she was forced to admit a great deal more than she wanted to.

"Shall I help you?" she offered, when she had given Giulia the necessary information. "I'm afraid there is rather a lot for you to do with so many people here."

If Giulia was surprised at this new air of command in Ruth, she took pains to hide it. With care, she corrected Ruth's Italian and made her repeat what she had to say several times over until she was word-perfect.

"If you permit, I shall get my sister to come in and help me until the Signor and Signora Roberto go back to Tunis," she suggested at some length. "She is accustomed to the ways of the house."

Ruth agreed that this would be an admirable arrangement, and then, having nothing else to delay her, she braced herself to go into the *salotta* to join the others. She could hear Mario and his mother laughing about something and wondered what it was. It was difficult not to feel excluded in a way by her presence, though she knew she was being ridiculous. Mary-Anne was the last person to be possessive over her son. But then it wasn't Mary-Anne's possessiveness that was the trouble, Ruth told herself wryly, it was her own!

"I have been telling Mario about my plan to have my own house," Mary-Anne told Ruth as she entered the room.

Ruth gave Mario a nervous look and dropped her eyes again. "If it were very near—" she began vaguely.

"Nonsense!" Mario exploded. "And you're not to encourage her, Ruth," he added angrily. "My mother will live in my house for as long as she stays in Sicily!"

"Then I shall go back to New York," Mary-Anne sighed.

"But how can you be any less lonely in a house by yourself?" Mario shot at her. "Ruth would make you very welcome here."

His mother gave him an unblinking look. "She already has," she said.

Ruth had a sudden inspiration. "Why don't you turn one wing of the house into a place of your own?" she suggested with a spurt of enthusiasm. "Then you wouldn't be far away, but you could be quite private whenever you liked!"

"There!" said Mary-Anne. "I told Mario you'd think of something!"

Mario looked at his wife and smiled. "You have found yourself an ally!" he observed dryly. "My mother thinks I am unkind to you—"

"Not *unkind*," Mary-Anne protested anxiously. "Just that you ask too much!"

"Do I?" Mario asked Ruth directly. She made a flustered movement, quite unable to answer.

"You know you do!" Mary-Anne rushed to Ruth's defence. "You haven't been at all gentle! Why, you've scared the girl half to death!"

Mario's eyes flashed with amusement. "Rubbish, Mamma! Ruth knows very well what I am about. She finds our customs a little strange at first, but then so did you when you first married my father!"

Mary-Anne looked severe. "But then I was in love with your father!" she pointed out delicately.

Mario smiled straight into his mother's startled eyes. "As Ruth is with me!" he said with complete certainty. "If you don't believe me, ask her!"

CHAPTER TWELVE

MARY-ANNE was tactful enough not to ask anything of the sort. She cleared her throat as if she was trying not to laugh and patted the sofa beside her, inviting Ruth to share it with her.

"I thought I'd be quite exhausted after all my travels," she said brightly, "but I'm not in the least bit tired. How would it be if we made up a party and went to the marionette theatre?" She looked meaningly at Roberto and Lucia. "When did we last go anywhere together?"

"That's true," Lucia agreed. "When you left to go to New York, you were still in mourning." She looked at her sister-in-law with the faintest disapproval in her eyes. "Have you left off wearing black completely?"

"Why not?" Mary-Anne said affably.

Lucia sighed. "It is hardly more than a year—"

"I don't need black to remind me of that!" Mary-Anne said with decision. "That is one of the few things that I refuse to be Sicilian about! Why, what with friends and relations dying more and more often as one gets older, one would never get out of black at all!"

"It seems like that sometimes," Lucia agreed. "I am in black now, so perhaps I shouldn't go and see the marionettes?" She cast an anxious look of inquiry at Roberto. "I do so want to go!" she added.

"Then go we shall," Roberto agreed heavily. He was still confused by the events of the day and more than a little afraid that someone was going to ask him why he had been helping Ruth to leave Sicily without

Mario's knowledge or consent. "The three of us will go!" he added.

Ruth licked her dry lips. "But—but I'd like to go too!"

"We'll go tomorrow!" Mario promised her. "If you still want to go."

"Why shouldn't I want to?" Ruth asked him sulkily.

His laughing eyes met hers. "I'll tell you the answer to that later!" he said.

There was some argument amongst the three elder members of the party as to what they wanted to see. Mary-Anne preferred the violence of the battle to any opera and, finally the other two gave way in the face of her determination.

"They are fantastic!" she told Ruth with enthusiasm. "Sicilian puppets are the best in the world! They make them so well! They're about two feet high, but they can do *everything*! I just love to see them lowering their visors and crashing into battle. They do the sound effects so realistically as well, with all the operators stamping about behind the scenes. Before I saw them, I used to think that I didn't like puppets, but these are as good, or better, than any live theatre. You must make Mario take you—" She broke off, a trifle embarrassed. "Some other time, of course," she went on quickly. "Oh, my dear, it is awkward for you having so many people about—" As this was so much worse than what she had been going to say in the first place, she subsided into an uncomfortable silence.

"When we go to Tunis tomorrow, I am sure Ruth will miss us very much!" Lucia put in, unable to believe that anyone could not want to have their whole family about them every minute of the day.

Ruth smiled. "So I will!" she assured her.

"Who else will take you to Luigi's for your hair and

explain things to you?" Lucia asked innocently. "Of course you will miss me!"

"You will always be welcome to visit us in Tunis," Roberto added kindly.

Ruth was warmed by the genuineness of their affection for her. "I'd like that," she said.

"We'll both come," Mario agreed. "The very first holiday we take!"

The evening was a success, there was no doubt about that! Roberto, Lucia, and Mary-Anne had changed into full evening dress for their visit to the puppet theatre and they looked truly magnificent as they gathered round the table for the evening meal. Ruth had tried to persuade Mary-Anne to take her seat opposite Mario, but her mother-in-law would not.

"I know," she had said, "that on the Continent a married couple will often sit side by side at the table, but the Verdecchios have never done so. You must sit at the top of your table, my dear. It's only proper."

And so Ruth had sat down opposite Mario, so placed that she had only to raise her eyes to see him whenever she would. It was tempting, she found, to watch him all the time : to follow the expressions as they flitted across his face, and to admire the hauteur that his large, broken nose gave him in repose. She herself could eat practically nothing. In the most ridiculous way, although she managed to look quite calm on the surface, she was suffering from butterflies in her stomach. It was something in the way Mario looked at her from time to time and, even more, the knowledge that once the others had gone out, he was bound to insist that the time had come for them to come to some sort of an understanding. The very thought of the kind of understanding he might insist on gave her a nervous feeling that nothing would quell.

She made a gallant effort at light conversation all

through the first course. It was strange, she thought, how one was able to divide one's mind in two, keeping the surface for polite chatter, while the underneath was frozen into immobility by sheer fright and worry.

"P-Pearl doesn't like travelling much on her own," she said in answer to a polite remark of Roberto's. "She doesn't know any language except English and, if people don't speak that, she feels cut off."

"And what languages do you speak?" Mary-Anne asked her languidly.

Ruth coloured a little in case she should be thought to be boasting. "I can speak French quite well," she said. "I spent last winter learning Italian at evening classes, but I—but—"

"Ah!" Mario teased her gently. "So that's why you insist on referring to me in the third person! I shall have to teach you the proper way to address your husband!"

Ruth blushed violently, but she had perfect control over her voice as she answered: "We were told we wouldn't have the need to be anything other than formal."

"I knew the moment I set eyes on you that you had led a sheltered life!" Mario riposted.

"So you repeatedly said!" she told him bitterly.

He looked at her with warm amusement. "I wonder why you should resent it?" he questioned lightly.

She felt a strong desire to laugh. "It was the beginning of all my troubles, you may remember!" she said.

His eyes held hers, although she would have preferred not to be so open to him. "So that's what you think," he said.

But at last the meal came to an end and Roberto went to get the car while the women prettied themselves and fetched their wraps against the cool of the evening.

"We shall be very late," Mary-Anne told her son. "Don't wait up for us," she added meaningly.

He grinned at her and went out with them to help them into the car and to say goodnight to his uncle. Left to herself, Ruth would have liked to have taken refuge in the kitchen with Giulia, but Giulia scorned her help with the washing up. It was obvious that she didn't really like having anyone else in her kitchen, a point of view that Ruth was bound to respect, and so she wandered back into the *salotto*, with Saro following close at her heels.

She was fidgeting with the flowers when Mario came back. He stood in the doorway, watching her for a few minutes in silence. She saw him finally and the colour flooded into her cheeks, although she gave no other sign that she had noticed him.

"That is a very matronly occupation!" he said with a smile.

"*Matronly!*" she repeated. "Oh, Mario, how could you?" She gurgled with laughter. "You are the most uncomplimentary beast I've ever met!'

"I knew we should get back to your sheltered life sooner or later," he said in resigned tones.

She lifted her chin. "It wasn't as sheltered as all that! I'm not saying that most of the men we knew didn't prefer Pearl, but I did have some boy-friends of my own!"

"And the pleasant knowledge that they were the ones who could see further than their own noses!" he suggested.

She was shocked. "How can you say such a thing?" she demanded of him. "And that's something that *I* want to talk to *you* about! I think you owe Pearl an apology for the way you've treated her!"

He raised his eyebrows. "Indeed?" he said haughtily.

"Yes, *indeed*!"

"I can't see that she has any cause for complaining. I think I've been very nice to her—"

"But you shouldn't have been!" Ruth told him hotly.

"I can't think why not!"

She could think of several reasons, but none of them were ones that she felt able to discuss with him.

"She's more vulnerable than you think!" she said desperately.

"And rather less so than you think," he answered.

Ruth cast him a wary look and very nearly ruined the whole flower arrangement by snapping off one of the blooms right at the top of the stem. Mario reached out a hand and took the remaining flowers out of harm's way. In doing so, he somehow managed to capture both her hands in his and drew her gently across to the sofa, sitting her down beside him.

"Suppose you tell me what sent you rushing off to England," he suggested.

"I can't!" she said baldly.

His hand tightened on hers. "Am I supposed to guess?" His voice was charming, but inflexible.

"It's all so silly!" she exclaimed. "I can't imagine how I allowed myself to be put in such a ridiculous position!" She gave him a petulant look and was immediately sure that he would make her regret it. "You must see that the only way you can get rid of me is to let me go home!"

"I must be very obtuse," he said gently, "but I can't remember that I ever said I wanted to be rid of you."

"You didn't," she acknowledged.

"Then it was something I *did* that gave you this unfortunate idea?"

"No, of course not! But nobody wants to be married to someone he doesn't know—D-does he?"

183

"Perhaps not," he agreed.

Ruth bit her lip, completely miserable. "So there you are! You don't have to be!"

He leaned back, looking at her out of lazily smiling eyes. "But I had the oddest feeling that I knew you very well from the first moment I saw you," he said in mild, conversational tones.

She was much shaken. "In—in Naples?"

He looked surprised. "No, *not* in Naples! In Naples, I am sorry to say, I hardly noticed you at all. You stood in the hotel foyer and glared at me in the most shrewish manner. If I felt anything at all, I felt rather sorry for Pearl having to face you every time she came in from a date!"

"Oh?" Ruth said coldly.

He smiled. "I didn't know then that far from swooning if a man were to kiss you, you would kiss him right back!"

"Oh, I *didn't*!" she denied with considerable indignation.

He put his hand under her chin and forced her to look at him. "How can you tell such lies?" he mocked her.

Very easily, she assured him mentally. "Well, if I did, it was only because you took me by surprise," she said grudgingly.

He laughed. "And that is an even more shocking thing to say!" he reproved her.

"Besides," she added primly, "you said you never refused a challenge and I told you I didn't either!"

"Oh, I see! You were meeting a challenge! How strange that you should immediately run away!"

She gave him a look of pure dislike. "I *hate* you!" she told him fiercely.

He pulled her into the circle of his arms and she

184

was surprised to discover that she was more than comfortable with her head on his shoulder and with her hands tucked into his.

"More lies?" he asked her with so much laughter in his voice that her indignation died a sudden death, no matter how hard she tried to resuscitate it. She tried to sort out the chaotic thoughts that went through her mind and ended with hoping very much that he was shortly going to kiss her again.

"Is my mother right?" he asked when it was quite clear that she was too engaged in her own thoughts to go on arguing with him. "Do I ask too much of you?"

Ruth struggled for a long moment with her conscience. It seemed base to tell him that he did, when she knew that anything less would have been unworthy of them both. It was that that made her previous friendships with any man seem trivial by comparison. *I strove with none, for none was worth my strife!* Nor had they been! They had passed by without leaving so much as a ripple on the even tenor of her days. Only with Mario it had been quite different. From the moment he had come into her bedroom she had been lost. First he had made her laugh and then he had tormented her : lastly, he had kissed her and she had been vanquished! There was no denying that she had fallen very deeply in love with him.

"Well? Do I ask too much?" he prompted her.

It would be different if he had fallen in love with her too, but he hadn't. *Was* it too much to ask of her? That she should love him so completely and gain in return his interest, his children, and his wretched Sicilian honour? No, she admitted to herself with honesty, it was not too much. She would rather anything than not have him at all.

"Well?" he prompted her again.

A smile trembled on her lips. "No," she admitted, "you don't ask too much?"

"Not more than you have to give?"

"No."

"Then you are content to stay here as my wife?"

She nodded, aware of a constriction at the back of her throat. "Yes," she said.

"And be the mother of my children?"

"Y-yes."

She felt a tremor of laughter run through him. "And be the typical Sicilian wife with nothing better to do than to seek the approval of her husband?"

"I suppose so," she said with such marked reluctance that he was hard put to it not to laugh outright.

"*And*," he said provocatively, "allow me to kiss any pretty girl who comes my way?"

That was too much! "No!" she flared up. "I will not! You are *my* husband—" His laughter was too much for her. She snatched her hand out of his and made a wild swipe at him, but he was far too strong for her. In a flash he had both her hands caught in his and pinned them behind her in the small of her back.

"I daresay," he said, laughing straight into her face, "that you are the only pretty girl I shall want to kiss! Vixen!"

He let her hands go as his lips met hers. She thought he would crush her ribs and she gave a little sob of protest. He was not much more gentle after that, but for some reason she no longer seemed to notice. Her hands crept up behind his shoulders and she pulled him closer still. What did it matter that he was not in love with her? If he could kiss like this, and this, she must be happy!

Giulia knocked on the door, which set Saro off barking. Ruth pulled herself together with difficulty and sat bolt upright, with her hands clasped in her lap, while Mario went to the door to see what the maid wanted.

"My sister is agreeable to coming in in the morning," she called to Ruth from the open door.

"Oh? Good," said Ruth.

Giulia looked from one to the other of them, her eyes sparkling. "I'll say goodnight, *signore, signora*! Shall I lock up before I go?"

"Please do," said Mario.

Giulia came further into the room, making a great deal of noise as she relentlessly checked that each and every shutter was properly secured for the night.

"I'll leave the front door for Signor Roberto," she assured them cheerfully. "I have no doubt they will be late back!"

Mario leaned against the doorpost, watching the two women with amusement. He didn't seem to mind at all that Giulia knew he had been kissing her, Ruth thought resentfully. To him, it seemed perfectly natural that he should kiss his wife when and where he would, but she was not yet ready to face the world—as *his wife*! But why not?

She stood up, feeling decidedly weak at the knees.

"I—I think I shall go upstairs to bed," she managed.

"So early?" Mario demurred, his voice quivering with laughter.

Giulia frowned at him. "It has been a long day for the Signora," she reminded him reproachfully. "She will be feeling lost with her sister gone! You go to your bed, *cara*! I have turned down the bed for you ready and laid out your nightdress—"

Ruth thanked her briefly and fled, with Saro snapping at her heels, delightedly whirling round in circles, quite sure that she was about to do something exciting and unusual.

"Be quiet, you beastly animal!" she berated him.

Saro barked the harder.

"You'll be in the stables!" she warned him.

"Now that," Mario drawled from the foot of the stairs, "would be an excellent idea!"

Ruth gave him a harassed look. She snatched the dog up into her arms and rushed headlong up the stairs, his laughter following her all the way.

He came through the door without knocking, wearing a truly magnificent dressing-gown that filled her with envy.

"You weren't wearing *that* the other day!" she accused him.

"If I had known it was you here, and not Pearl, I might have done," he said with an air of candour. "I don't think it would appeal to Pearl—"

"How can you say so?" she asked with exaggerated sarcasm.

He smiled at her and she was obliged to concentrate hard on her breathing until she felt more normal.

"M-Mario—" she began.

He sat on the edge of the bed beside her. "My love?" he responded immediately.

"I wish you wouldn't call me that!" she said crossly.

"I'll call you whatever I please," he answered.

"But it isn't *true*!"

He looked surprised. "And that matters?"

"N-no," she said hesitantly.

He looked at her closely. "I was right, wasn't I? You do love me?"

"You know I do," she said in a small, tight voice. He took her hand in his, playing with the ring on her finger. "That was generous of you," he said gently.

Ruth pulled her hand away from him. "No, it wasn't!" she denied fiercely. "You knew that I loved you. I don't know how it happened, but I wouldn't have married you otherwise—only *I* didn't know it then! I just thought I'd gone mad! And anyway," she went on, her sense of grievance getting the better of her, "I didn't have any choice! It wasn't at all a comfortable position to be in."

"It would have been even more uncomfortable if you hadn't fallen in love with me," he pointed out reasonably.

"Why?" she demanded sulkily.

"Because I should have kissed you just the same!" he told her.

She blushed and was immediately cross with herself for doing so. "Pearl *never* blushes!" she said in despair.

"No?" He sounded amused.

"It's—it's a very awkward habit!" she said bitterly.

"I think it's a charming one," he answered. "Very proper in a loving bride!" he added, for the sheer joy of watching the colour slide up into her cheeks again.

"D-don't!" she protested.

He laughed. "You *darling*!" he exclaimed.

Ruth was shocked by this form of address. She gave him a nervous look and hastily looked away again. The familiar amusement was very apparent in his dark eyes, but there was something else as well, far more unnerving, something she would have liked to have explored, but hadn't the necessary courage.

"Mario, was it true? Did you *indeed* have to marry me?"

"It's the custom," he replied.

She sighed. "Then you wouldn't have married me otherwise?"

"No."

She looked at him again. "It doesn't matter," she said.

"I wouldn't have married you *then*," he went on, just as if she hadn't spoken.

"Th-then?" she repeated.

"I would have found some other way to keep you here," he added reflectively, "until you had time to grow used to me!"

Her eyes widened. "I—I d-don't understand," she stammered.

He looked amused. "Don't you? Then I'll tell you, my love. The day I walked through that door and found you sleeping in my bed—"

"It wasn't your bed!" she denied indignantly.

"In *my* bed," he repeated firmly, "it was a great shock to my system. I didn't particularly want to get seriously involved with anyone! But one look at you, and there I was!"

Ruth looked at him, fascinated. "Wh-where were you?"

"Involved!"

She frowned. "W-were you?"

"I came through that door and there you were, bursting with righteous indignation! I knew the instant I set eyes on you that I should have to keep you there for ever, you were so completely *right*! You were made to be my wife! Happily, you had placed yourself in the position where you didn't have any choice!"

Ruth thought that she had never had such a fascinating conversation with anyone! "I shouldn't have thought you'd like a reluctant wife very much," she said.

"There wasn't too much danger of that!" he retorted.

She lifted her chin pugnaciously. "That isn't kind!" she told him.

"No, it wasn't," he agreed repentantly. "But the fact of the matter is, my dear, that it never occurred to me that I couldn't make you love me!"

"You chose a very odd way of going about it," she said flatly. "You had to have your own way about *everything*!"

"And that rankles?"

She came near to laughter. "No," she admitted, "but it *might* have done! You made me give everything, even my pride. I might have hated you for that!"

"Was pride the reason you ran away?"

She nodded unhappily. "Oh, Mario," she said, "I love you so much! I was afraid I'd be unhappy if I didn't have anything in return. I wasn't sure you even *liked* me! When I came home from the vineyards with Henry and you kissed me and I thought you *knew*, I couldn't bear it!" She took a deep breath. "I'm not asking you to love me," she went on bravely, "at least, not very much, but if you think you could pretend sometimes—" Her eyes met Mario's and she stopped in a hurry. "M-Mario?"

"Ruth *darling*, I've spent the greater part of the evening telling you that I love you! LOVE you, do you hear me? How can you make such an outrageous suggestion?"

She blinked, uneasily aware of her heart thudding inside her.

"I thought we'd spent the greater part of the evening establishing that I loved you!" she said faintly, her courage fast evaporating as he reached out for her. She thought he was going to shake her, but he didn't, he kissed her very gently on the lips.

"Have I made a mull of it?" he asked her humorously. "How could you think that I wanted you to be a loving wife, if I didn't love you? It's because I love you that I want our love to be the central thing in both our lives—"

"It is, in mine," she said unsteadily.

He looked at her in wonder, a slight smile on his lips. "*Carissima*, would you really have given me your life without my love?"

"I thought it was what you wanted," she answered simply.

When he kissed her she felt that she had come home. How could she ever have thought that he didn't love her? She laughed with sheer happiness against his lips.

"*This* is what I wanted!" he whispered in her ear. "Oh, Ruth, you little darling, I love you to distraction!"

She didn't answer him because she couldn't. She didn't need to answer him. He was the sum of her pride, her life, her love, because he had made her his wife.